"It all could have gone so terribly wrong."

"But it didn't."

She caught her lower lip between her pretty white teeth. "I was so scared."

"Hey." He brushed a hand along her arm, just to reassure her. "You're okay. And Munch is fine."

She drew in a shaky breath and then, well, somehow it just happened. She dropped the purse. When she reached out, so did he.

He pulled her into his arms and breathed in the scent of her skin, so fresh and sweet with a hint of his own soap and shampoo. He heard the wind through the trees, a bird calling far off—and Munch at their feet, happily panting.

It was a fine moment and he savored the hell out of it.

"Garrett," she whispered, like his name was her secret. And she tucked her blond head under his chin. She felt so good, so soft in all the right places. He wrapped her tighter in his arms and almost wished he would never have to let her go.

* * *

THE BRAVOS OF JUSTICE CREEK:
Where bold hearts collide under Western skies

Dear Reader,

Many of my stories are really about learning to follow your heart. Sometimes you need to say no to a relationship that isn't working. But knowing when to say yes matters most of all—to be able to greet love with open arms when it finds you, no matter how long that might take or how many wrong turns you've made in your own personal road before you find the one whose heart answers yours.

Garrett Bravo considers himself a workaholic who's no good at relationships. But then kooky heiress Cami Lockwood stumbles into his mountain getaway and the staunchly single CEO can't get enough of the endearing, irrepressible runaway bride.

Cami is definitely following her impulsive, wide-open heart at last, after years of trying to be what her wealthy family expects her to be. She's busting out and claiming a life that's just right for her now. And nothing and nobody will get in her way.

Garrett adores her pretty much on sight. She brightens his days and heats up his nights. He'll do anything for her—except admit that she's the woman for him. Garrett doesn't trust his heart.

But Cami's no quitter. One way or another, she'll make him see that they were meant to be together.

I hope Cami and Garrett's story makes you smile and warms your heart.

Happy reading and all my very best,

Christine Rimmer

Garrett Bravo's Runaway Bride

Christine Rimmer

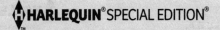

Recycling programs
for this product may
not exist in your area.

ISBN-13: 978-0-373-62374-7

Garrett Bravo's Runaway Bride

Copyright © 2017 by Christine Rimmer

Printed in U.S.A.

Christine Rimmer came to her profession the long way around. She tried everything from acting to teaching to telephone sales. Now she's finally found work that suits her perfectly. She insists she never had a problem keeping a job—she was merely gaining "life experience" for her future as a novelist. Christine lives with her family in Oregon. Visit her at christinerimmer.com.

Visit the Author Profile page
at Harlequin.com for more titles.

For MSR.
Always.

Chapter One

When the battered bride staggered into the circle of firelight, it was after nine at night, and Garrett Bravo was sitting outside his isolated getaway cabin slow-roasting a hot dog on a stick.

For a weirdly suspended moment, Garrett knew he must be hallucinating.

But how could that be? He'd never been the type who saw things that weren't there. And he'd only had a couple of beers.

His Aussie sheepdog, Munch, let out a sharp whine of surprise.

"Munch. Stay." He glanced sternly down at the dog, who quivered in place and stared at the apparition on the other side of their campfire.

Garrett looked up again. She was still there.

He opened his mouth to speak, but nothing came

out. Finally, with a ridiculous shout of confusion and lingering disbelief, he jumped to his feet. The sudden movement knocked his hot dog off the stick and down to the dirt. He gaped at it as it fell. Munch cocked an ear and glanced up at him expectantly. When he failed to say no, the dog made short work of the fallen treat.

"Oh, really," said the tattered vision in white. She came around the fire toward him, waving a grimy hand. "You don't need to get up. It's worse than it looks, I promise you."

It looked pretty bad to him. Leaves decorated her straggling updo and nasty bruises marred her smooth bare shoulders and arms. Her left eye was deep purple and swollen shut. The poor woman's big white dress was ripped in several places and liberally streaked with mud. And her bare feet? As battered as the rest of her.

"My God," he croaked. "Are you sure you're all right?"

She blew a tangled hank of blond hair out of her good eye and shrugged. "Well, I've been better."

How could she be so calm? Had her groom gotten violent? If so, the man deserved a taste of his own damn medicine—and speaking of medicine, she needed a doctor. He should call for an ambulance, stat. He dropped his hot-dog stick on top of the ice chest by his chair and dug in a pocket for his phone.

But the phone wasn't there. Because he'd left it in the cabin. Up here on the mountain, cell reception was nil.

Garrett let out a long string of bad words and then demanded, "Who did this to you?"

The bride remained unconcerned. She hitched a

thumb back over her shoulder. "Little accident back down the road a ways."

"Your groom…?"

"Oh, he's still in Denver. Some stranger ran me off the road." As he tried to process that bit of news, she added, "Camilla Lockwood. But please call me Cami." She offered a scratched, dirty hand.

Numbly, he took it. It felt cool and soft in his grip. *And real.* She was definitely real. "Garrett. Garrett Bravo."

"Good to meet you." A frown tightened the skin between her eyes. "You okay, Garrett? You look a little pale."

He looked pale? "How will I call you an ambulance when my phone doesn't work?"

"You won't." She reached up, clasped his shoulder and gave it a reassuring squeeze. "It's fine, really. I don't need a doctor."

"But—"

"Take my word for it, I would know. You think this looks bad?" She indicated her body with graceful sweeps of both hands. "I've been through worse. Lots worse—and who's this?" She dropped to a crouch, her giant dress belling out around her, and held out a hand to his dog. Munch made a questioning sound. "Come on, sweetie pie," she coaxed. When Garrett made no objections, Munch let out a happy little bark and scuttled right over. "Oh, aren't you the cutest boy?" She scratched his ears, rubbed his spotted coat—and glanced up at Garrett with a beaming smile. "Beautiful dog. Such pretty markings." Garrett dipped to her level, took her arm and pulled her to her feet again. "Hey!" She tried to jerk free. "Ease up."

"We need to get you down the mountain."

"No, we don't."

Ignoring her protests, he started pulling her toward his Jeep Wrangler Rubicon on the far side of the cabin.

"Garrett. Stop, I mean it." She dug in her heels.

"Camilla, come on now."

"I said, call me Cami. And no. Just no. I'm not going anywhere." As she whipped her arm free of his grasp, he debated the advisability of scooping her up and carrying her bodily to the Jeep. But even with all the scratches and bruises, she seemed to have a lot of fight left in her. And say he did manage to get her over there and into the SUV. How would he convince her to stay put while he ran into the cabin for the keys?

Maybe he could reason with her. "You need a doctor. I only want to take you down the mountain to Justice Creek General."

"No means no, Garrett." She braced her hands on her hips and narrowed her one working eye to a slit. "And I have clearly said no."

So much for reason. "Will you at least sit down? Rest for a minute?"

She flipped that same tangled hank of hair off her forehead. "Sure."

Before she could change her mind, he caught her elbow and dragged her over to his chair. "Here. Sit." She dropped to the chair with a large huff of breath, her big dress poofing out as she landed, then quickly deflating. Slowly and gently, he explained, "Relax, okay? I'm just going to go into the cabin and get the first aid kit."

"First aid can wait."

"But—"

"Please, Garrett." She picked a twig from her hair and tossed it over her shoulder. "I need water. My tongue's just a dried-up old piece of leather in my mouth, you know?"

That tongue of hers seemed to be working pretty well to him. But yeah. Water. He could do that. "Stay right there?"

"I won't move a muscle." Munch, always a sucker for a pretty girl, sidled close and plunked down beside the chair. For the dog, she had a tender smile. "Hey, honey." She stroked his head. "What's his name?"

"Munch."

"Cute," she said. And Garrett just stood there, staring down at her as she petted his dog. Finally, she glanced up at him again and asked hopefully, "Water?"

"Right." Against his better judgment, he left her alone with only Munch to look after her as he ran for the cabin. At the door, he paused with his hand on the knob. What if she took off?

Well, what if she did? If she insisted on wandering Moosejaw Mountain in the dark barefoot in her torn-up wedding dress, far be it from him to try to stop her.

He went in, filled a tall insulated bottle with water, grabbed the dish towel and ran back out.

She was still there. "You're a lifesaver," she said when he handed her the bottle.

He flipped open the cooler, grabbed a handful of ice and wrapped it in the towel. "For your eye."

She took a long drink and then let out a happy sigh. "Thank you." Only then did she accept the ice. Pressing it gingerly to her bad eye, she frowned. "Don't tell me I stole your only chair." She started to rise.

"Relax." He patted the air between them until she

dropped back into the seat. "I've got a spare." He grabbed the extra camp chair from where he'd left it leaning against a tree, snapped it open and set it down on the other side of the cooler from her.

Now what?

Awkward seconds struggled by as they just sat there. She sipped her water and iced her eye and he tried to decide what he should do next.

Maybe she needed food. "Are you hungry, Cami?"

She gave a long sigh. "Starved."

He could help with that at least. "How about a hot dog?"

She rewarded him with a radiant smile. "A hot dog would really hit the spot about now."

A half an hour later, the beat-up bride had drunk two bottles of water and accepted three hot dogs, each of which she'd shared with Munch. The dog remained stretched out beside her. Periodically, he would lift his head from his paws to gaze up at her adoringly.

Garrett still felt bad that he hadn't convinced her to let him drive her to the hospital. She could have at least allowed him to get out the first aid kit and sterilize a few of those scratches.

He asked glumly, "Do you have a head injury?"

She repositioned the makeshift ice pack on her injured eye. "And you need to this know why?"

He shrugged. "I was going to offer you a beer. But if you've got a concussion, maybe not."

That earned him another dazzling smile. "A beer would be so perfect."

Apparently, she was never going to answer the head

injury question. But she seemed reasonably clearheaded, so he flipped open the cooler and passed her a beer.

Tucking the ice pack into the cup holder on her chair, she popped the top and giggled like a happy kid when it foamed. He watched her throat move as she swallowed, after which she settled back in her chair and stared up at the star-thick Colorado sky.

She really did seem okay. And at the moment, he couldn't think of any more ways she might let him help her. He settled back, too.

Somewhere in the trees, a night bird twittered.

Cami made a soft, contented little sound. "Got to hand it to you, Garrett. This is the life."

He completely agreed. "Yeah. Munch and I have been up here for almost two weeks now, only driving down the mountain twice for food and supplies. The first few days were tough. I kept worrying about work. But eventually, I got over that and started enjoying the quiet and the big trees. Overall it's been great."

"So you don't live up here?"

"No. I'm on vacation. I've got three more days. Wednesday, I have to head home."

"To?" She stared up at the sky, the beer can dangling from one hand as she idly scratched Munch's back with the other.

"I live down in Justice Creek."

Cami said dreamily, "I've been to Justice Creek a couple of times. Such a pretty little town."

"I grew up there. My sister and I run a construction company."

"What's your sister's name?"

"Nell. She's a pistol." He rolled his head Cami's way

again and found her watching him. Otherworldly, the gleaming blue of that good eye. "You would like her."

Cami's dirty angel's face looked wistful. "A pistol, huh?"

"Oh, yeah. Nell never did a damn thing she didn't want to do. She's unpredictable, but you can count on her, too. I always know she has my back."

"She sounds amazing." Cami turned her face to the stars again. "I wish I could be like that." Garrett was about to tell her she was more than unpredictable enough, when she glanced down at her torn dress and said in a small voice, "I'm thinking you've already guessed that I ran out on my wedding." She slanted him a glance. At his nod, she faced the sky again and continued. "Biggest wedding of the season. Everyone who's anyone in Denver was there. I was going to go through with it up to the very last moment—which means, I didn't plan my escape." She wrinkled her nose at the stars. "That's me. No planning. I never think ahead. When I can't take it anymore, I just freak and run. Today, that happened during the wedding march. My bridesmaids were already on their way down the aisle. The wedding planner signaled me out of the bride's room…" Her voice trailed off.

He prompted, "And then?"

"And then I just grabbed my purse off the vanity table and sprinted out the back door. The door opened on the parking lot and I'd made my dad drive me in my car for the ride to the church." A low, sad chuckle escaped her. "Okay. I confess, I may have done a little planning, after all. Because I had a spare set of keys in my purse. I jumped in my BMW and took off with no plan after that whatsoever and nowhere in particular to go." She paused for another sip of beer.

When she settled back again, she continued. "Eventually I got out on the highway. I took an off-ramp. I saw the sign to Moosejaw Mountain. I took that turn. It's one twisty road getting up here, Garrett, but my 750i handled like a dream. I would still have that car if some idiot in a green pickup hadn't come barreling down as I was going up. Ran me right over the side of the road and into a very steep ravine."

"My God." Had she been knocked out, then? He probably shouldn't have given her that beer.

She raised the beer in question toward the distant moon and took another swallow. "I admit, it was scary while it was happening."

"Were you knocked unconscious?"

"No. But the airbags deployed and somehow, I got smacked in the eye. When the car finally stopped rolling, I couldn't get the door open. And that, along with everything else—how messed up my life had gotten, the way I'd run out on my wedding that never should have been happening in the first place—well, it all just made me tired. So I took a nap."

"A nap," he echoed disbelievingly. "In a wrecked car at the bottom of a ravine?"

"That's right." She was defiant. "I closed my eyes and went to sleep—and you should see the way you're looking at me. Same way my parents do. Like you wonder how much brain damage I've sustained. And you don't even know about the coma."

He gulped. "There's a coma?"

She waved a dismissing hand. "That was six years ago. Yeah, there are scars. But I'm fully recovered—

well, I mean, as much as anyone can recover from an experience like that. Anyhoo, back to the ravine. Whoever was driving that green pickup didn't bother to stop or call for help, so when I finally decided I really had to make the effort to get out of the car and get back up to the road, I was on my own."

"That driver should be arrested. Did you get a plate number?"

She gave him a look of great patience. "Sorry, Garrett. I was kind of busy trying to keep from rolling off the side of the road. And then I did roll off the road. And then I just gave up for a while and took a nap. When I decided to get moving again, it took me a long time to get the car door open. And scrambling up out of there? That's where most of these scratches and bruises came from. It was not the most fun I ever had, believe me. But I finally got back up to the road. I stood there and thought, down or up? I'd already been down, so I started climbing. I just kept walking until I got here."

"We should be calling the police on that guy in the pickup. Leaving the scene of an accident is a crime."

"Too bad your phone doesn't work." She didn't sound the least regretful.

He tried one more time to get through to her. "If you'd just get in the Jeep, we could—"

"Uh-uh. I really am okay, Garrett. And I like it here. I'm free at last and I'm not going anywhere until I'm ready to go. No one runs my life but me. Not ever again." She offered another toast with her beer can. "From this day forward, I decide where I go and when I'm leaving. Okay, I didn't handle my escape very well. Yes, I ran away like I always do. I left Charles at the altar and I'm sorry about that."

"Charles is your fiancé?"

"*Was* my fiancé. Charles and I grew up together. His parents and my parents are good friends. He and I are both vice presidents at my family's company, WellWay Naturals."

Garrett had heard of WellWay. Their products were in all the big grocery stores. "The vitamin company?"

She nodded. "Vitamins, supplements and skin care products. Charles has been after me for years to marry him. I kept telling him no. Eventually, though, he wore me down. I messed up, I know it. I handled the whole thing really badly, but at least I didn't marry him, and someday he'll thank me." She blew out a weary breath. "And yes, I ran away again. But this time, I *own* it. This time, I'm laying claim to my future. I'm going forward now, not back."

"Forward to…?"

"When I figure that out, you'll be the first to know." She drank, plunked the empty can on the cooler between them and granted him another gorgeous smile. "So then." She grabbed the ice again and reapplied it to her eye. "You know my story. What brings *you* to this beautiful neck of the woods, Garrett?"

Is she actually out of her mind? he wondered. Could be. But for some reason, he *liked* her. He went ahead and told her the embarrassing truth. "I'm kind of hiding out."

"I can relate. Who are *you* hiding from?"

"My mother."

"What did she do to you?"

"It's what she's *trying* to do. The past few years, she's been obsessed with seeing me and my sisters and brothers happily married. Nell and I are the only ones still single. Even my mother knows better than to try to tell Nellie what to do. So lately Ma's been pestering *me*."

"Pestering you, how?"

"Demanding I come see her and then browbeating me when I get there about how it's time I found love and happiness at last. Introducing me to very nice women I don't want to go out with. Lecturing me about 'trying again' every chance she gets."

"Again?"

"I was married. Years ago. It didn't work out. I suck at relationships." Cami chuckled. He shot her a frown. "That's funny?"

"It's just the way you said it…"

"What way?"

"Really fast, like you wanted to get it over with and you didn't want me to ask you any questions about it."

"I did. And I don't."

"Duly noted." She poked at her black eye, wincing a little, and then iced it some more. Her ring finger was bare.

"You lost your ring."

She shook her head. "Before I left the church parking lot, I took it off and stuck it in the glove box. I'm guessing it's still there. Go on, about your mother and your needing to get away?"

He shrugged. "Long story short, I'm kind of a workaholic and I needed a break from everything, my mother most of all. So I'm here where my mother would not be caught dead—roughing it in a one-room cabin on top of a mountain. And she can't even call me because there's no cell service."

Cami clucked her tongue, chiding him. "You seem way too pleased with yourself when you say that."

"I kind of am. Unfortunately, to appease her, I did promise her I'd have dinner with her the night I get back to town. But I'll deal with that when it happens. For now, Ma's off my back and I'm up here in the great wide-open, taking a breather, trying to figure out what to change up to get more out of life."

"Well, Garrett. What do you know? We have stuff in common."

For the first time since she'd materialized out of nowhere, he allowed himself to laugh. "I guess we do."

"And I sure am glad you were here." Cami was picking bits of crushed, dried leaves out of her hair with her free hand.

"You look tired." At his softly spoken words, she made a cute humming sound that might have been agreement. He asked in a coaxing tone, "You ever gonna let me patch you up a little?"

Cami worked another leaf free of her tangled hair. He accepted that she wouldn't answer. But then she did. "I would kill for a bath about now."

"That can be arranged."

Cami decided she loved Garrett's cabin.

On the outside, it was simple, of weathered wood with old-fashioned sash-type windows and a front porch with stone steps.

Inside, it was cozy and plain, just one big living area with the kitchen on one wall, the bed on another and a sofa under the front window.

When he ushered her ahead of him into the dinky

bathroom, she grinned and brushed a finger along the wooden rim of the tub. "It's half of a barrel."

"That's right, a whiskey barrel." He hung back in the doorway. There wasn't enough room for both of them in there. "A full-size tub wouldn't fit." He was tall and broad-shouldered with beautiful light brown eyes that made her think of melting caramel. Definitely a hottie, with a few days' worth of scruff on his lean cheeks, dressed in old jeans, dusty hiking boots and a faded brown denim jacket over a white T-shirt. He was so easy to be with. Already, she liked him a lot and had to keep reminding herself that she hardly knew him.

"I put in the tub and hot water up here this spring," he said. "Before that, it was sponge baths or nothing."

She glanced around at the vintage sink, the milk-glass light fixture and the knotty-pine paneling. "I like it. It's super rustic."

He indicated the metal caddy hooked on the outside of the tub. "Soap and shampoo are right there. Towel and washcloth under the sink. There's a new tooth-brush and a comb you can use in the medicine cabinet. I'll go back out to the fire and leave the window over the sofa open. Give me a holler if you need anything."

"Would you undo the hooks at the back of my dress before you go?"

"Uh, sure." He took a step into the tight space and she backed up to meet him.

Gentle fingers brushed the skin between her shoulder blades and then worked their way down. She pressed the dress to her chest to keep it from falling off. "All done," he said after a minute.

She looked over her shoulder and met those melty

eyes. "Take this thing?" To her, the dress represented all that was wrong in her life. It wasn't even her style, so poufy and traditional. Her mom had coaxed her into choosing it. "I don't think there's room for both it and me in here."

He had soft lips to go with the melty eyes. Those lips turned up slightly. "Uh. Sure." He was looking at her kind of funny, like he still didn't quite know what to make of her—which was nothing new. People often looked at her that way. Maybe he was thinking she shouldn't be so quick to take off her dress in front of him.

Well, maybe she shouldn't. But then again, why not?

She trusted him. He'd been nothing but kind to her, helping her all he could while at the same time respecting her wishes. Never once had he bullied her to do things his way. This man was not going to make a move on her—or if he did, he'd already proven that he understood the word *no*.

Cami dropped the dress. It plopped around her feet like a parachute, belling out, then collapsing. Underneath, she wore a tight white satin bustier that ended in ruffles at her hips. She'd thrown her silk stockings away back down the mountain somewhere. There hadn't been much left of them after she dragged herself up to the road. As for her five-inch Louboutins and her giant half-slip covered in a big froth of tulle? She'd dumped those during the trek up out of the ravine.

The bustier, with satin panties underneath, covered her as well as a swimsuit would. It also showed the long, pale scar cutting down the outside of her right thigh—but she'd never been the least sensitive about that. She considered it a war wound, proof of an earlier attempt to escape a life that was always a prison for her.

Stepping free of the acres of dirty white lace, she held it up to him. "Burn it, will you?"

He took it gingerly. "What will you wear?"

"I don't even care." Unfortunately, she'd left her suitcases in Denver—turned them over to Charles yesterday to load into the limousine. She had nothing but the dress and her underwear, but she would go naked before she put that thing on again. "Burn it."

"Up to you." Garrett backed into the main room and shut the door.

Cami turned to the barrel tub and flipped on the taps.

Garrett had just doused the fire for the night when he heard the cabin door open.

Munch ran up the steps to greet their surprise guest as she emerged from inside wrapped in a towel. The light from the cabin outlined her curvy shape in gold as she knelt to give Munch the attention he'd come looking for.

As Garrett mounted the steps, she rose. "Thank you. Really. I feel so much better now."

"Good—and it's past midnight. You think you could sleep?" With a soft sound of agreement, she turned and went back inside. He and Munch followed her. Garrett shut the door.

She faced him with a sigh. "Did you burn it?"

"It's nothing but ash." He dropped to the old bentwood chair by the door and started taking off his boots.

When he looked up again, she was still standing there wearing a wistful smile. "Thanks."

"Any time. You want one of my shirts to sleep in?"

Her smile turned radiant. "Yes, please."

He got a faded Pearl Jam T-shirt from the dresser and handed it over.

"Thank you. Again." She disappeared into the bathroom, emerging in the shirt that covered her to midthigh.

There was another awkward moment and it came sharply home to him that he didn't know this woman at all. They were two strangers about to share the same sleeping space.

"I'll just take my turn in the bathroom." He eased around her, went in and shut the bathroom door. Hanging on the back of it next to his sweats was that sexy corset thingy of hers. It struck him all over again how bizarre this whole situation was.

When he came back out wearing the sweats, she'd already stretched out on the couch. She was settling his old afghan over herself.

He moved a few steps closer. "Cami, take the bed."

"No way." She wiggled her toes under the blanket and adjusted the thin throw pillow under her head. "This couch isn't big enough for you and we both know it. Your feet would be hanging off the end." Munch made himself comfortable in the space between the rickety coffee table and the sofa. She put her hand down and stroked his spotted coat. "Don't look at me like that. I'm not budging."

"Suit yourself."

"Oh, yes, I will. From this day forward, I will be suiting the hell out of myself, just you watch me."

He got the extra pillow from the bed and gave it to her. "You're allowed to change your mind. If you can't sleep on those lumpy cushions, I'll trade with you."

She yawned hugely. "'Night." Pulling the afghan up under her chin, she shut her good eye.

In the morning, her black eye had opened to a slit and she refused a fresh ice pack for it. "It'll be fine," she assured him. "I'm a fast healer."

He put a couple of logs in the woodstove to get the coals going again and made coffee and scrambled eggs. She shoveled it in like she hadn't eaten in weeks, and he felt ridiculously pleased with himself to be taking good care of her.

But then he said, "After breakfast, I'll drive you down the mountain."

She guzzled some coffee. "You said you were staying for three more days."

"Cami, you really need to—"

"Uh-uh." She showed him the hand. "Don't say it. Don't tell me what I need. For the rest of my life, *I* decide what I need. And what I need is to stay here with you and Munch until you have to go."

"But you—"

"Not going. Forget it. I need a few more days up here in the peace and the quiet before facing civilization and calling my parents to say I'm all right."

"They're probably really worried about you."

"I know." She chewed on her plump lower lip and looked away. "And I feel bad about that. But right now, I need this—you and me and Munch up on this mountain with nothing to do but breathe the fresh air and appreciate the big trees." He marshaled his arguments, but then she leaned across the rough surface of the table and begged him, "Please, Garrett. Please."

And he could not do it—could not tell her no. "Damn it," he muttered.

"Thank you," she replied, extra sweet and so sincere.

He got up to pour them more coffee. "So then, what *do* you want to do today—besides breathing and staring at trees?"

She dimpled adorably. "I'm so glad you asked. See, I left the church without my suitcases, but I did have my purse, with my credit cards and my driver's license. I don't know what I was thinking when I finally got my car door open and started climbing up to the road. I left my purse behind. I was hoping we might go back for it."

Garrett gave her his flip-flops, another shirt and a pair of his jeans to wear, with an old belt to keep them up. She wore that corset thing under the shirt for a bra. He knew this because he was a man and thus way too aware of what went on beneath a woman's shirt.

They piled in the Jeep, with her riding shotgun and Munch in his favorite spot all the way in back. More than halfway to the state road at the base of the mountain, she said she thought they'd passed the place where she went into the ravine. He turned around the next chance he got.

She found it on the way back up, recognizing a Forest Service fire danger sign a few yards from where she'd gone off the edge. There was enough of a shoulder to park by the sign.

Before he could tell her to leave the dog in the Jeep,

she let him out. Panting happily, Munch followed her to the edge.

"This is definitely the place," Garrett said, taking in the skid marks. He came up beside her and peered over the edge. Her car had flattened everything in its path as it went down. It seemed impossible that she'd survived the crash and the tumble into the ravine. "You were lucky to be driving that Beemer."

She made a sound of agreement. "Handles like a dream and one of the safest cars around. I'm going to miss it."

"I can see the car." The vehicle was half-buried in underbrush, but twisted metal and shiny red paint gave it away. "What's that?" He pointed at something white and poufy halfway down.

"My slip. It was hard enough climbing with the dress. I kept tripping, so I took it off and left it."

"You want it?"

She looked at him, her expression severe. "No, I do not."

The incline was close to eighty percent. It would be steep going, but there were lots of trees and bushes to hold on to. He figured he could make it down there, get whatever she wanted from the car and get back up without too much trouble. "Anything else you want besides your purse?"

"There's a notebook and some pens in the glove compartment. I would really like to have those—oh, and my engagement ring should be in there, too. I should give it back to Charles."

"Anything else?"

"My old red hoodie might be in the trunk. I could use that, if we can get it open—oh, and there's a hatch through to the trunk in the back seat, so maybe…" She let her voice trail off on a hopeful note.

"I'll try. Take Munch and wait in the Jeep."

"What?" She set her stubborn chin. "I'm going with you."

Had he expected that? Yeah, pretty much. "Not in my flip-flops that don't even fit you. Your poor feet are cut up enough already."

"But I—"

"Stop, Cami. It's not a good idea and I think you know it's not."

"It just seems wrong to make you go alone."

"I'm dressed for the job and you're not. It'll be simpler and safer if I do this myself."

She mouthed a wistful thank-you at him and turned back to the Wrangler. "Come on, Munchy." With a happy whine, the dog jumped in.

"This shouldn't take long," he reassured her as she climbed up to the seat and pulled the door shut.

He started down. It was not only steep, the ground was thick with roots, rocks and debris. Past her big, white slip, he found one white satin shoe and then the other. The soles were red, the high heels covered in dirty rhinestones. Cami hadn't asked for them, so he left them where they lay.

The car was upside down and badly bent and battered, the driver's door gaping open, the trunk crushed in. The cab, though, was intact. He pushed the deflated air bags out of the way and looked for a purse, finding it easily—on the ceiling, which was now the floor. Most of the contents had escaped.

Checking not only the ceiling but under the upside-down seats, he found the latest model iPhone, a hot-pink leather wallet full of cards and cash, plus loose makeup, a comb, a brush, a tin of Altoids and all the other random stuff a woman just has to cart around with her wherever she goes. He shoved it all back in the purse.

The glove box popped right open for him, spewing its contents, including the pens and notebook she'd mentioned. He found her registration and proof of insurance in there, too. He even found her fancy ring. It had a platinum band and a large, square-cut diamond. The ex-fiancé might not have been the guy for her, but at least he wasn't a cheapskate. He stuck the ring in his pocket.

Finally, he managed to crawl into the back seat and get the trapdoor to the trunk open. After a little groping around back there, he got hold of the hoodie she'd asked for.

The purse was more of a satchel, big enough that he could stick the notebook, pens and car documents in there, too. He tied the sleeves of the hoodie around his neck, shoved the straps of the satchel up his arm as far as they would go and crawled from the wreck.

He'd made it halfway back up to the road when he heard Munch frantically barking, followed by a bizarre, pulsing cry.

Adrenaline spurting, every nerve on red alert, Garrett froze in midstep. He knew that strange cry. Black bears made that sound when you stole their food or otherwise pissed them off.

Chapter Two

Dropping the purse, grabbing for branches to pull him forward, Garrett scrambled as fast as he could up the hillside. Somewhere up ahead Munch barked like crazy and the bear's angry vibrating yowl continued.

Then Cami's voice joined in. "Shoo! Back! Get out of here, you!"

Garrett grabbed the slim trunk of a cottonwood sapling and hauled himself higher, finally getting close enough that he could see them through the brush. They were maybe ten yards below the road. Cami had lost the flip-flops but had found a long stick. She held off the bear with it while Munch ran in circles around them, barking.

With no weapon handy, Garrett grabbed a rock and threw it at the bear, striking it on the rump. The bear turned and let out a quick growl in Garrett's direction, but then went right back to chuffing and growling at Cami, pawing the ground.

She yelped in response and kept jabbing with her stick. "Back! Go!" Munch continued circling them, barking frantically.

Garrett scuttled closer and threw a bigger rock.

That did it. The bear turned on him. Black bears could move fast when they wanted to. And that one flew down the hill straight at him.

"Garrett!" Cami's terrified scream rang through the trees as Garrett lunged to the side, counting on gravity and the bear's forward momentum to drive it right past him.

It worked. The bear saw him move but couldn't stop in time. It lost its footing and started to roll.

A split second later, Munch zipped by, too.

"Munch!" Garrett shouted. "Stop!"

But the dog was already out of sight down the ravine. He heard the bear make that threatening sound again. There was scrabbling in the brush and grunting from the bear.

And then a loud, startled cry from his dog.

The bear gave another angry grunt. Brush rustled and branches snapped. Garrett caught a flash of dark fur through the undergrowth—the bear running off.

And then there was silence.

"Omigod!" Cami came sliding down the bank toward him. "Munchy! Oh, no!" She toppled.

Garrett caught her before she could fall. "Hey now. Hold on." With a gasp, she blinked up at him. He asked, "You all right?"

"Let me go." She tried to break free. "I have to—"

"No," he said softly. When she kept struggling, he shouted it. "No!"

A whimper escaped her. "But Munch…"

He took her by the shoulders. "Go back to the Jeep."

"I can't—"

"Look at me, Cami. Look at me now." She moaned, but she focused. "Whatever happened down there, it's over. Don't believe what you see in the movies. Black bears as a rule aren't aggressive and that one's already run off."

"But where's Munchy?"

"I'll go see."

"Oh, Garrett. I was going to stay in the Jeep, I promise. I'm so sorry." Tears filled her good eye and seeped from the injured one.

"It's okay. Just let me—"

"God, I feel so terrible. Munchy started barking. He jumped right over me and out the open window."

"He probably caught the bear's scent. We had a couple of bears messing with our trash on a camping trip once. Munch was only a pup, but he chased them away. Just doing his job, that's all."

"If anything has happened to him, I'll never forgive myself."

He gave her shoulders a gentle shake. "Look at me. Listen. It's not your fault."

"But I—"

"I'm sure he's fine." No, he was not sure. But he had to say something to settle her down. Last night, he would have sworn that nothing could shake her, but right now he feared she might lose it completely. "I need to get down there and see what's going on, okay?" She swallowed hard. And then, finally, tear tracks shining on her too-pale cheeks, she nodded. He instructed, "I want you to wait right here. Do that for me. Please?"

"Yes." The agreement came out of her on a whisper of sound. And then more strongly, she added, "Okay."

"Come on now. Over here..." He guided her to a boulder that poked up from the bracken and slowly pushed her down. "I'll be right back," he promised. She just stared up at him, tears dripping from her chin.

What else could he do? He took her hoodie from around his neck. It zipped up the front, so he wrapped it around her. "You going to be okay?"

She sniffled and stuck her hand in a pocket of the hoodie. "Go," she commanded, pulling out a rumpled tissue and dabbing her eyes. "I'm fine."

He wasn't so sure about that, but he turned anyway, and started down the bank, passing her purse where he'd dropped it. Several yards farther on, he spotted Munch's tail sticking out of a clump of brush.

His whole body went numb, a strange coldness creeping in, freezing him in place. He'd worried that Cami might break. Now, the sight of that unmoving tail almost broke *him*.

And then that tail twitched.

"Munch?" He practically fell the rest of the way.

Landing hard on his knees, he shoved the brush aside.

The poor guy was just lying there, as though he'd stretched out on his side for a nap.

"Munch?"

There was a weak little whine. And then, woozily, Munch lifted his head.

"Munch. Munch…" For some reason, Garrett couldn't stop saying the mutt's name. He bent close. No blood that he could see.

The dog whined again.

"How you doing, boy? Where does it hurt?" Garrett ran seeking fingers over head, neck, back, belly and down the long bones of each leg. He checked the paws, too.

Nothing.

About then, Munch gave his head a sharp shake.

"You okay, buddy?" The dog wriggled his way upright and started wagging his tail.

Relief poured through Garrett, bringing another wave of weakness. He plunked back on his butt in the brush and grabbed the dog in a hug. "Guess you're all right, after all, huh?"

For that, he got sloppy doggy kisses all over his face.

Laughing, Garrett caught Munch's furry mug between his hands. The dog whined sharply. Garrett felt it then, a bump behind the right ear. Carefully, he stroked the sore spot. "You think you can make it back up to the Wrangler?"

The dog let out a sound that just might have been *Yes!*

Garrett rocked to his feet and straightened with care. His legs still felt shaky, but they were taking his weight. "Well, let's go, then. Heel."

Munch obeyed, falling into step at his left side. Eager to reassure Cami that the dog was okay, Garrett climbed fast, pausing only once to grab her purse as they passed it.

A moment later, he caught sight of her waiting on the rock where he'd left her, wearing the hoodie, looking like a lost Little Red Riding Hood, tears shining on her soft cheeks. She spotted him. Batting tears away, she sat up straighter. And then she saw Munch. With a gasp, she shot to her feet. "He's okay?"

Garrett gave her a nod. "Go ahead. Show him the love."

"Munchy!" she cried. The mutt raced to greet her and she dipped low to meet him.

Garrett waited, giving her all the time she wanted to pet and praise his dog. When she finally looked at him again, he explained, "The bear must have whacked him a good one. When I found him, he was knocked out, but I think he's fine now."

She submitted to more doggy kisses. "Oh, you sweet boy. I'm so glad you're all right…"

When she finally stood up again, he handed over the diamond ring and that giant purse.

"Thank you, Garrett," she said very softly, slipping the ring into the pocket of the jeans she'd borrowed from him. "I seem to be saying that a lot lately, but I really do mean it every time."

"Did you want those high-heeled shoes with the red soles? I can go back and get them…" When she just shook her head, he asked, "You sure?" He eyed her bare feet. "Looks like you might need them."

"I still have your flip-flops. They're up by the Jeep. I kicked them off when I ran after Munch." For a long, sweet moment, they just grinned at each other. Then she said kind of breathlessly, "It all could have gone so terribly wrong."

"But it didn't."

She caught her lower lip between her pretty white teeth. "I was so scared."

"Hey." He brushed a hand along her arm, just to reassure her. "You're okay. And Munch is fine."

She drew in a shaky breath and then, well, somehow it just happened. She dropped the purse. When she reached out, so did he.

He pulled her into his arms and breathed in the scent of her skin, so fresh and sweet with a hint of his own soap and shampoo. He heard the wind through the trees, a bird calling far off—and Munch at their feet, happily panting.

It was a fine moment and he savored the hell out of it.

"Garrett," she whispered, like his name was her secret. And she tucked her blond head under his chin. She felt so good, so soft in all the right places. He wrapped her tighter in his arms and almost wished he would never have to let her go.

Which was crazy. He'd just met her last night, hardly knew her at all. And yesterday she'd almost married some other guy. She could seem tough and unflappable, but she'd had way too much stress and excitement recently. The last thing she needed was him getting too friendly with her.

Gently and way too reluctantly, he set her away from him. Biting that plump lower lip again, she gazed up at him, her expression both hopeful and a little bit dazed.

"Now, listen." He ached to stroke a hand down her

pale hair, to cradle her soft cheek in his palm, but he didn't. "What do you say I take you back down the mountain? We'll be in Justice Creek in less than an hour and you can—"

"Stop." In an instant, that dazed, dewy look vanished. Her soft mouth pinched tight. Without another word, she grabbed her purse and headed for the Jeep, Munch at her heels.

Garrett followed at a distance as she climbed up to the road. He gave her time to stick her feet in his flip-flops and usher the dog in on the passenger's side. When she jumped up to the seat and slammed the door, he circled around the front of the vehicle.

As soon as he got in behind the wheel and pulled the door shut, she commanded, "Take me back to the cabin or I'll say goodbye right here."

He let the silence stretch out before coaxing, "Come on. Don't be that way."

Her tight mouth softened a little. "I'm sorry. I'm just not ready yet to deal with all the crap that's waiting for me back in the real world."

"I meant what I told you," he warned. "I'm going home Wednesday."

She turned her gaze from him and stared blankly out the windshield. "I understand."

"Cami, when I go, I'm not just leaving you alone in that cabin. You don't even have decent shoes to wear."

"I know." She looked so sad.

And he had that need again, to touch her in a soothing way—to clasp her hand or pat her shoulder. Or better yet, to pull her into his arms where she felt so good and fit just right. But he kept his hands to himself.

He spoke firmly. "If I take you back to the cabin

now, you have to agree that you'll be ready to go down the mountain with me on Wednesday."

"I'll be ready." She met his eyes then. "I'll go when you go. I just need a few more days on this mountain of yours where no one can find me."

He eyed the faded, baggy T-shirt he'd given her to wear, the jeans she had to hold up with a battered old belt and the too-big flip-flops that had to be a real pain to walk in. "How 'bout this? We drive down to town and get you some clothes that fit you, then come right back up to the cabin?"

Her lush mouth got pinchy. "Nice try. I'm not going down there till Wednesday. I'm just not. I want this time away from everything, Garrett. And I'm going to have it."

"We can use my credit card if you're worried they'll—"

"No."

"Well, then, I could take you back to the cabin and then go down myself and get you some better clothes."

"Better clothes can wait till Wednesday." Her pinched look had softened. "Please. Will you just let it go?"

He figured it was about the best deal he was going to get from her. "Fair enough," he said gruffly. And he had to hand it to her. She'd picked the right place to disappear. No one was likely to come looking for her up here.

She was smiling again, her good eye a little misty. "You are the best."

"Sure."

"I mean it. You are."

"So how come I have so much trouble telling you no?"

"Don't be a grump about it." She slapped at him playfully. "I happen to love that you can't tell me no. My parents and Charles never had a problem with no when it came to me. It was always 'Camilla, no' and 'Camilla, don't' and 'Camilla, behave yourself and do what *I* say.' I've spent my whole life doing what other people think I should do, interspersed with the occasional attempt to escape their soul-crushing expectations."

Again, he had to quell the urge to reach for her. She was the cutest thing, with her black eye and her scrappy attitude. "Well, you're running your own life now."

"Oh, yes, I definitely am."

"And we have an agreement. We're at the cabin till Wednesday and then you'll let me drive you home."

"Got it." She stuck out her hand and they shook on it.

At the cabin, he had firewood to split.

She volunteered to help so he got the maul ax, his goggles and two pair of gloves and led her out to the chopping block behind the cabin. "I've never chopped wood," she said cheerfully.

He put on his goggles. "And you're not starting now. Not in flip-flops." A slip of the maul and she could lose a toe. "You can stack the split logs, if you want to." He pulled on his work gloves and handed her the extra pair. "But take it slow and be careful."

"I will."

For a couple of hours, he worked up a sweat with

the ax. He tossed the split logs away from the chopping block. She gathered them up and stacked them against the back wall of the cabin. Then when lunchtime approached, she went inside to make sandwiches. He washed up at the faucet behind the cabin and joined her on the front steps where she had the food waiting.

They ate without sharing a word, but the silence was neither tense nor awkward. Just easy. Relaxed. After lunch, he went back to splitting wood.

When he came to check on her later, she was sitting in one of the camp chairs drawing pictures in her notebook.

He peeked over her shoulder at a pencil sketch of Munch snoozing at her feet. "You're good at that."

"I wanted to go to art school," she said as she shaded in Munch's markings, the beautiful spots and patches of his blue merle coat. "I always dreamed of studying at CalArts. But my father prevailed. I went to Northwestern for a business degree and took a few art classes on the side. Then, the summer I graduated from college, I knew I had to do something to make a life on my own terms."

"But your dad wasn't going for it?"

"No, he was not. I tried to make him understand that I didn't want to work at WellWay, that I needed a career I'd created for myself. He just wouldn't listen."

"What about your mother? She wouldn't step up and support you?"

"My mother never goes against my dad." She shaded in Munch's feathery tail, her pencil strokes both light and sure. "And she basically agrees with him, anyway."

"So you went to work at WellWay, then?"

"No. I tried to get away again."

"Again?"

"There were several times I ran before that. The time I ran after college, I packed up my car and headed for Southern California—and was rear-ended by a drunk driver on I-70 in the middle of the night."

Garrett swore low, with feeling.

"Yeah. It was bad. I almost died."

"That coma you mentioned last night...?"

She nodded but didn't look up from her drawing of Munch. "I was unconscious when they pulled me from the wreck and I stayed that way for two weeks. You probably wondered about that scar on my leg? Another souvenir of that particular escape attempt."

"But you made it through all right."

"Thanks to the best medical team money could buy and a boatload of physical therapy, yes, I did."

He had that yearning again to touch her. To pull her up into his arms and comfort her, though she didn't seem the least upset.

He was, though. Just hearing about how bad she'd been hurt made something inside him twist with anger—at her father, who wouldn't let her live her own life. And at her mother, too, for not supporting Cami's right to be whatever she wanted to be.

"When I was well enough to go home, I moved back in with my parents." She kept her head tipped down, her focus on the notebook in her lap. "My father insisted. And I was too weak to put up a fight. There was more physical therapy—and the other kind, too, for my supposed mental and emotional issues. And when I'd completely recovered from the accident and finished all the therapy, I moved to my own place at last—and started my brilliant career at WellWay."

He clasped her shoulder and gave it a squeeze, because he couldn't stop himself.

She didn't lift her head from her focus on the sketch, but she did readjust the sketch pad on her knees enough to give his hand a pat. "It's okay, Garrett. I'm all better now."

Feeling only a little foolish, he let go.

She sighed. "Mostly, I like to create my own comic strips." She flipped the sketchbook back a page to a cartoonlike sequence of sketches where a cute little bunny with a ribbon in her hair used a stick to fight off a bear with the help of a patch-eyed Aussie dog. A boy bunny in jeans and a T-shirt similar to Garrett's ran toward the girl bunny wearing a freaked-out expression on his face.

"I'm guessing that's me?"

She slanted him a teasing glance. "Okay. I took a little artistic license. You didn't look *that* scared."

"Maybe I didn't look it, but *that* scared is exactly how I felt."

A giggle escaped her. "Yeah. Well, it's not like you were the only one." She flipped the page back and continued working on the drawing of Munch. "I have a whole series on the bunny family. Unlike my real family, the bunny family works on their issues. They respect each other and try to give each other support and enough space that every bunny gets what she wants of life."

"Wishful thinking?"

"Oh, yeah."

He watched her draw for a while. But there was

more wood to split, so he went on around back and got busy with the maul.

Later, he showed her how to lay and light a campfire. They had steaks and canned beans. When they went inside, he taught her the basics of how to use a woodstove.

She took another bath. When she came back out to the main room, she smelled of soap and toothpaste. "Anything good to read around here?"

He pulled a box full of paperbacks out from under the bed. "Help yourself."

She chose a tattered Western and stretched out on the couch with it. When she fell asleep, he pulled the afghan over her and turned out the light.

The next day was pretty much the same, quiet and uneventful. She drew cartoons in her notebook. He split wood.

Beyond getting the wood in, he'd been planning an overnight hike and some fishing for these last couple of days on the mountain. But now that he had Cami with him, he didn't want to leave her alone for too long.

Strangely, it was no hardship to have to stick close to the cabin for her sake. There was just something about her. He felt good around her, kind of grounded. She pulled her weight and she didn't complain about the rustic living conditions.

They went for a walk up the road—not too far, about a mile. With only his flip-flops to wear, her feet couldn't take a real hike. They stopped at a point that looked out over the lower hills, some bare and rocky, others blanketed in pine and fir trees.

"Kind of clears your mind, being up here." She sent

him one of those dazzling smiles and he marveled at what a good time he was having with her. He would miss her after he dropped her off in Denver.

Was he growing too attached to her?

Oh, come on. He'd known her for less than forty-eight hours. No way a guy could get overly attached in that time.

That night, he tried to offer her the bed again. But she insisted she was comfortable on the couch.

After he turned out the light, he could hear her wiggling around, fiddling with her pillow, settling in. "You sure you're okay over there?"

"Perfect." She lay still. The cabin seemed extra quiet suddenly. Outside, faintly, he heard the hoot of an owl. There was a soft popping sound from the stove as the embers settled. "Garrett?"

"Hmm?"

"Tell me about you."

He smiled to himself. It was nice, the sound of her voice in the dark. "What do you want to know?"

"Well, your parents. What are they like?"

So he told her about his father, Frank, who'd had two families at the same time—one with his wife, Sondra, with whom he had two sons and two daughters. And the other with Garrett's mother, Willow. "Ma had three boys, me included, and two girls with dear old dad. And then, when Sondra died—the day after her funeral as a matter of fact—my dad married my mom."

"Ouch—I mean, wow, that was fast."

"No kidding. Everyone was pissed off about it, that my dad couldn't show just a hint of sensitivity to Sondra's memory, that Ma couldn't wait a little longer after all those years of being my dad's 'other woman.' At the time, we were all pretty much at war, me and my mother's other kids on one side, our half siblings on the other."

"It sounds awful."

"Yeah. But eventually we all grew up and realized it wasn't *our* fault that our parents couldn't manage to behave responsibly and respect their marriage vows. Now we're tight. We all like getting together, looking out for each other, knowing we can count on each other, all that family stuff. My half siblings are even nice to my mother, which I find really impressive. Not only is she the woman my dad cheated on Sondra with, she's not a friendly person. She's distant, hard to get to know."

Cami made a low, thoughtful sort of sound. "Are your mom and dad still together?"

"They were until he died six years ago. Now, when she's not traveling, which she does a lot, she lives alone in the mansion he built for Sondra, just her and the housekeeper."

"That sounds kind of sad."

"You'd have to meet her. She's not someone people feel sorry for. Like I said, she comes off kind of cold and superior. And then there's the whole matchmaking thing I mentioned the other night. She's driven us kind of crazy with that crap lately."

"Because she loves you and wants you to be happy."

He grunted. "Right. I'll keep telling myself that."

"And I did the math. Your dad had nine kids total?"

"That's right." Garrett laced his hands behind his

head and stared up at the shadowed rafters overhead. "You sound impressed."

"I kind of am. And jealous, too. I always wanted at least a sister. Preferably two. And I would have loved to have a brother. I truly do believe that if my parents had only had more kids, they wouldn't have been constantly on my case to do things their way. More kids keep the parents busy, you know? The parents have to chill a little and accept that they don't have absolute control."

"But you've finally broken free, right? You're going to do things your way now."

"Oh, yes, I am." She said it gleefully. "I'm finally going to find work that makes *me* happy. And I'm fortunate that I won't have to take just any job to get by. My trust fund matured three years ago, when I was twenty-five. I have my own investments and a good chunk of change in savings, too. My life is my own from now on."

"You really think your dad might have tried to cut you off just to get you to do what he wants?"

A silence from her side of the room. From the rug by the sofa, the tags on Munch's collar jingled as he gave himself a scratch. The sound was followed by a soft doggy sigh.

When Cami finally spoke, she didn't really answer his question. "Well, it doesn't matter if he would or he wouldn't. He can't. My money is my own. I'll be able to support myself while I figure out what *I* want to do with my life from now on." She sounded both wistful *and* determined.

He wanted to get up and go to her, pull her into

his arms and promise her that from now on her life was going to be downright amazing. He wanted to…

He cut the thought off before he got to the end of it.

He liked her. A lot. But she was going home to Denver and he was going back to Justice Creek. This, right now, in the cabin, just the two of them? It was only one of those things that happened sometimes. She'd needed some help and he was willing to give it.

They got along great and he enjoyed her company.

But that was all there was to it. Day after tomorrow, he would drive her down the mountain and that would be the end of it.

Tuesday pretty much flew by.

And that night in the dark, they talked some more.

She said she liked it on the mountain so much, she just might find a getaway cabin of her own. "Eventually. You know, after I figure out where I want to live and what to do with my life."

Garrett opened his mouth to tell her she could use the cabin any time she wanted to—and then caught himself before the words could escape.

It only *felt* like he'd known her forever. Tomorrow, he would take her home. Maybe he'd talk her into giving him her number. Who could say what would happen from there?

For now, though, offering her the use of his getaway cabin whenever she wanted it was going too far.

In the morning after breakfast, they loaded up the Jeep with Garrett's clothes, his camping stuff and the leftover food. He turned off the hot water, drained the tank and shut off the water to the cabin, too, just in case he didn't make it back up the mountain before winter set in. He unplugged the fridge and braced the door slightly open. Then he locked the cabin up tight.

At the Jeep, Cami paused to take in the plain, unpainted structure with its narrow front porch and red tin roof. "I'm going to miss this place."

Garrett couldn't stop himself from reaching out a hand to cradle the side of her face. Her black eye was open now, most of the swelling gone, though it was still a startling blend of black, brown and purple fading into green. She gazed up at him solemnly.

"I've loved having you here," he said.

Her throat moved as she swallowed. Her soft lips parted. He had no idea what she was going to say.

And he decided it would probably be wiser not to find out. "Come on. Let's get moving." He dropped his hand from her cheek and opened the door for Munch to hop in.

She didn't say much on the drive down the mountain. That surprised him.

He realized he'd been bracing for some kind of resistance from her. But she was quiet and accepting, her thoughtful gaze focused on the winding dirt road ahead.

Was she *too* quiet?

He hoped she was okay, that she hadn't started to stew over what would come next.

"So, Denver, then?" he asked when they approached the turnoff.

"You know," she said casually, "just take me to Justice Creek, if that's okay."

"But I thought—"

She cut him off with an airy wave of her hand. "No, really. I'll rent a car and drive myself back when I'm good and ready. But for now, I think I'll try Justice Creek for a while."

"Uh, you will?" Not only was he surprised at her abrupt change of plans, but he was suddenly ridiculously happy, which alarmed him a little.

"Yeah. I'll get a hotel room. Do you know a good place?"

He eased onto the state highway going west, toward Justice Creek. As he made the turn, he decided he couldn't just leave her at some hotel. "How about this? Come to my place first. We'll drop Munch off and put the food away and then we can, you know, talk about your options…"

The smile she gave him made the sunny day even brighter. "That sounds like a great idea. Your house, it is."

Cami's heart swelled with gratitude.

Garrett Bravo was not only hot and way too handsome, he was a good guy. A real-life hero, a hero who'd been up there on Moosejaw Mountain just when she needed a hero the most. Someday she would figure out how to repay him.

No, she had no idea where she was going or what she would do when she got there.

But so what? She was finally playing life by ear and loving every minute of it, following her instincts for once, the way she'd always longed to do.

Her condo in Denver was already on the market. At some point, she'd have to pack everything up and move it all to wherever she ended up living. But none of that had to be done right away.

First things first. She needed to get going on the rest of her life.

Whatever that might turn out to be.

The state highway became East Central Street as they entered the town of Justice Creek. They passed the town hall and Library Park on the right. Charming shops lined the street on either side.

Cami had always thought Justice Creek was a great place. With Denver only a ninety-minute drive away, the pretty little town at the edge of the national forest made a perfect day-trip destination. Cami had visited several times. She'd caught the summer rodeo once and shopped the annual Christmas fair the last four years running.

Every time she'd come to town, she'd felt right at home.

And now, today, with her life wide-open in front of her, Cami saw Justice Creek for what it was: a perfect jewel nestled in its own small valley, surrounded by spectacular mountains. The kind of place where a person like her might be happy to settle down.

They passed the turn to Oldfield Avenue. She glanced out her side window and saw the white walls and red tile roof of the world-famous Haltersham Hotel. It was perched on a rocky promontory with gray, craggy peaks looming above it.

Right then, with the magnificent old hotel in her sights, Cami experienced a moment of great clarity.

No wonder she'd ended up with Garrett and Munchy on Moosejaw Mountain. Her subconscious had been leading her right here to Justice Creek the whole time.

This town…

Oh, definitely. *This* was the town for her.

It was all so simple, so perfect and clear. The question of where she would live the rest of her life was already answered, had *been* answered long ago. The truth had only been waiting for her to be ready to see it.

Justice Creek would be her new home.

Chapter Three

A curving pebbled driveway led up to Garrett's house on Mountainview Avenue in Haltersham Heights not far from the hotel. The exterior was weathered cedar and shingles and silver-gray stone, with lots of big windows.

Inside, those windows let in plenty of light. The modern kitchen and dining room opened onto the living area. Two sets of glass doors led out to a low deck and a patio, complete with a fire pit.

"What a beautiful house." Cami set a box from the cabin on the gorgeous granite counter. It had a swirling pattern of cream, brown and silver. "Kind of modern and rustic, both at once." The vaulted wood ceilings had log accent beams.

Garrett opened the glass door by the table to let Munch out. "I had it built it a few years ago, when Bravo Construction really started making money."

She watched Munch bound off the deck and into the yard. "He won't run off?"

"There's a fence. He's fine."

Together, they brought in all the food. Garrett said he didn't mind her looking in his cabinets to see where things went, so she got to work putting the food away while he unloaded his clothes and a bunch of random camping equipment.

"I'm just going to get a load of laundry started," he said and vanished down the hallway off the kitchen.

Cami put boxes of crackers and cold cereal in an upper cabinet and then made herself march to the end of the counter where she'd dropped her Birkin bag on the first trip in from the garage. With a grimace of dread, she took out her phone. She'd fully charged it at the cabin and turned it off when they left.

As soon as she turned it on, there would be a flood of frantic calls, texts and messages to deal with. Up on the mountain, it had been so easy to tune out the real world. Not anymore. The time had come to deal with everyone she'd been trying not to think about. They were going to be very upset with her when they found out that she had purposely avoided dealing with them since Saturday afternoon.

She was still standing there with the powered-off phone in her hand when Garrett emerged from the laundry room.

"That is not a happy face." He put his arm around her.

She leaned into his solid strength, breathed in his woodsy scent and made herself smile up at him. "I think I'll just go out and sit on that back deck while I make a few calls."

"Anything I can do to help?"

Take me back up the mountain. We'll stay there forever, just you and me and Munchy. "Thanks, but I think this is something I need to deal with myself."

Garrett got busy putting his gear away in the garage.

When he returned to the kitchen, she was still outside, pacing back and forth across the wide patio tiles, the phone to her ear. Munch, panting anxiously, trailed along behind her. Garrett stood at the glass door admiring the shine to her thick gold hair. How could she be so pretty even in his ill-fitting old jeans and faded shirt?

When she glanced over and saw him watching her, she gave him a quick wave and went back to her pacing. It looked like the phone calls were going to take a while.

He finished putting the kitchen stuff away and made them some sandwiches. When she finally came inside, she went straight to the end of the counter and stuck her phone back in her giant purse.

"You made lunch," she said, her eyes worried, her smile way too bright.

"Come on." He pulled out one of the high padded chairs at the kitchen island. "Everything will look better after you eat."

She got up on the stool. "Yum. I'm so hungry."

He let her polish off half of her turkey on rye before he asked, "So. Want to talk about it?"

She gave a tiny shrug. "My parents are furious. They demanded I return to Denver immediately. I told them I'm not coming back except to close up my condo and pick up my stuff."

He touched her arm in reassurance. "I'm sorry, Cami."

"Yeah." She forced another sad little smile. "Me, too."

"How was it with Charles?"

"Not much better—scratch that. Worse. He said he had to see me immediately, that we *had* to talk."

"Don't let the guy bully you."

"I'm not. I told him I needed to think about the whole face-to-face idea. I made it clear that I wasn't coming back, so there really was no point in us meeting. He was calling me bad names when I hung up."

"What an ass."

"Well, I did leave the guy at that altar, after all."

"And now he wants to talk about that? What's the point?"

Now she was the one putting her hand on his arm. It felt really good there. "I don't know, Garrett. I mean, I love that you're on my side, but I do feel guilty about running away. It had to be pretty awful for him."

"Talking about it with him isn't going to fix anything."

"I know you're right. But as I said, I haven't decided whether to talk to him or not."

"If you do decide to see him, meet him here."

"Why?"

"I should be close by, just in case."

She patted his arm and then picked up the other half of her sandwich. "At least my maid of honor was understanding. She promised she'd call my other bridesmaids and tell them I'm okay. It's so weird." She stared thoughtfully down at the triangle of sandwich in her hands. "I *like* my maid of honor, but I never felt all that close to her. It's as if, in Denver, I was just going through the motions, acting out living a life that wasn't really mine—oh, and, apparently, I'm a missing person, so I guess I need to go see the police and explain how I'm not so missing, after all."

"That, I can definitely help you with."

"No way. You've done enough."

No, he hadn't. Not if she still needed him. And clearly, she did. "My brother-in-law, Seth Yancy, is the county sheriff. I'll take you to the justice center."

She crunched a tortilla chip. "Uh-uh. You have been beyond amazing, but I've got to start cleaning up my own mess. I'll go myself. There's a car rental place in Justice Creek, right? I'll call them and have them bring me a car. Then I'll go visit your brother-in-law the sheriff and explain that I'm not missing. Once that's handled, I'll get a hotel room. And *then* I'm going shopping so you can have your jeans, shirt and flip-flops back."

"Keep them." He took a bite of his pickle. "They look better on you, anyway."

She gave a cute little snort of laughter. "They look awful on me and we both know it."

Her laugh eased his concern for her a little. "So... You're staying here in Justice Creek?"

She studied the sandwich for a moment, then set it back down. "Yep. I've been trying to figure out how to tell you because it sounds kind of crazy, but I made my decision an hour ago, as we were driving along Central Street. In a blinding flash of insight, I realized that I love it here and that Justice Creek is the place for me—and you're giving me that look, Garrett."

"Which look is that?"

"Like you're wondering if I'm a few fries short of a Happy Meal."

Was he? Well, maybe. A little. He'd never met anyone like her, that was for certain. "I'm just surprised, that's all. But hey, I love my hometown, too. It's a good place to live."

Garrett got that she needed to start somewhere if she really was going to make a whole new life for herself. And why not Justice Creek? She would probably be very happy here.

And the more he thought about it, the more he disliked the idea of her checking into a hotel. He had four bedrooms and three of them were empty. Also, he felt protective toward her—which was perfectly natural, given the circumstances. He'd looked after her on the mountain and he wasn't ready to stop yet. She had a great attitude, but creating her life all over again from scratch would be challenging.

He had to keep her close for a while, to be sure she was handling things all right and be ready to step in if she needed his help. Especially if the ex-bridegroom showed up. She would have to have backup for that.

"Garrett?"

"Hmm?"

"What exactly are you thinking?"

He put it right out there. "Stay here at my house. I've got plenty of room."

She nibbled another chip. "I don't know. Didn't we just go over how I've taken way more than enough advantage of you already?"

"No, you haven't. Besides, what will Munch do without you?" The dog, stretched out on the floor near his food bowl, flapped his tail against the floor and gave a hopeful whine right on cue. "See? You're not even gone yet and he's already sad about how much he'll miss you."

"I'll miss him, too, but I have to go sometime."

Not yet, she didn't. The more he thought about it, the more sensible her staying with him seemed. "How 'bout this? Just play it by ear. Stay over tonight and decide tomorrow if you want to stay longer."

She answered his question with one of her own. "You finished?"

"All done." She grabbed both their plates and took them to the sink. Before she could trot out more reasons to leave, he said, "Give me your phone."

"Because?"

"We need to trade numbers."

She flicked on the faucet and gave the dishes a quick rinse. "It's in my purse."

He got the phone and sent himself a text, thinking how strange it was that he'd slept in the same room with her for the past four nights and he was just now getting her number. "Okay. We're set. Now let me show you your room, then I'll get you a key and write down the alarm code."

An hour later, Garrett had left to check in at Bravo Construction and the nice guy from the car rental place had just dropped off a cute little silver Subaru Forester.

Cami checked the car over and gave the guy her credit card to run through his reader. Another car pulled up and the guy from the rental place got in and left.

She was about to hop into the Subaru when she remembered that she hadn't locked the front door or armed the alarm, so she ran back up the steps to deal with that.

Munch was waiting just inside the door. He whined and wagged his tail. After a minute, she realized he was trying to lead her back to the kitchen. When she followed, he went straight to the glass door.

"You want to go out, Munchy?" He whined and panted up at her. She opened the door and out he went. Right then, the house phone on the end of the counter started ringing. There was absolutely no way it could be for her, but she checked the display, anyway.

Willow Bravo.

Garrett's mother…

Cami snatched the phone from the base because… well, she wasn't exactly sure why. Sometimes she didn't know what got into her lately. One moment she'd get a little down about all the ways she'd messed up her life. But then, in an instant, all this lovely new freedom had her feeling bold and ready for anything, and that had her doing things she wouldn't ordinarily do.

Like answering Garrett's phone for no reason except that she was curious about his mother. "Hello?"

For a moment, the line was silent. Then a cool, slightly husky voice said, "Hello, who is this?"

"My name is Cami Lockwood."

"Do I have the right number? I'm calling Garrett Bravo."

"Yes, this is Garrett's house."

"Put him on the line, please. Tell him his mother is calling."

Cami debated how much to tell the woman, given that Garrett had run off to his cabin partly to get a break from her. "I'm sorry. He's not here right now."

Another silence from Willow. Then she said, "Cami—it *is* Cami, right? I don't believe we've met. Are you from the cleaning service?"

"Yes, it's Cami. And no, I'm not the maid. I'm a friend of Garrett's."

"Oh, really?" Willow's tone had perked up. Given what Garrett had told her, Cami knew why. Willow thought she was Garrett's girlfriend. "A *new* friend, I'm guessing."

"A *special* friend," Cami added; she had no idea why, except that her friendship with Garrett *was* special. Just not in a romantic way.

"I'm so happy to hear that." Willow's tone said it all. Garrett's mom was making assumptions. Cami ought to stop her. But she didn't. Willow said, "I can't believe he's never mentioned you before."

"Yes, well, as you said, we, um, only got together recently." She was making it worse and she knew it.

But somehow, she couldn't stop.

"Cami, I can't wait to meet you. Do you live here in town?"

"I'm originally from Denver, but yes. For the time being, I'm staying with Garrett."

"Wonderful." The cool alto voice had warmed considerably. "Then he's home from the cabin today as planned?"

"Yes. We just got back a couple of hours ago. Now he's gone to check on things at Bravo Construction."

Willow actually chuckled. "You stayed at the cabin together? I had no idea."

"Well, it was sort of a spur-of-the-moment decision."

"But he never takes anyone up to the cabin."

"He didn't take me. He went on his own."

"But you said you were there together." Willow sounded confused. Understandably so.

Cami explained, "I, um, joined him a few days ago. And I do love it up there. It's so peaceful. I hated to leave." It was nothing but the truth. Just not *all* of the truth.

"I don't get the appeal of roughing it, frankly." Willow sounded downright chatty, as though she and Cami were already BFFs. "Give me a luxury resort with all the amenities, if you don't mind. But I do realize that any special friend of Garrett's would have to enjoy all that outdoorsy stuff—and listen, I won't keep you. The reason I called was to remind my son that we're having dinner tonight. Would you be sure to tell him that I'll expect him here at the mansion at seven?"

"Of course, I'll tell him."

"And, Cami, I have a great idea." Willow paused and then asked coaxingly, "Why don't you join us for dinner tonight?"

Cami opened her mouth to decline—but then again, she was living by her instincts now, wasn't she? And her instincts told her that if she played this right, she could repay Garrett just a little for everything he'd done for her. Because, come to think of it, what better way to get his mother off his back on the matchmaking front than for Cami to go to dinner with him? Already, Willow believed that she and Garrett were together in the romantic sense.

And okay, pretending to be Garrett's girlfriend would be dishonest. But in the end, who, really, could it hurt?

"Hello? Cami, are you still with me?"

"Right here."

"Perfect. We're on, then. See you both at seven."

She really did need to talk to Garrett before saying yes to that. "I... Wait. Willow, I'm not sure if... Hello? Willow?" But Willow had already hung up.

Cami set the phone very carefully into its cradle and then considered snatching it up again and calling Willow back.

Instead, she got out her own phone and called Garrett.

He answered on the second ring. "Hey. Everything okay?"

"Define okay."

"Cami." His voice was suddenly harder. Darker. "Just tell me. What's going on? Is it that idiot, Charles?"

"No, really," she rushed to reassure him. "It's nothing about Charles."

"Well, then?"

She dragged in a big breath and let it all out in a rush. "Your mom called to remind you of dinner at the mansion at seven tonight. I told her I was staying here and that I am your special friend and then she invited me to dinner tonight, too."

There was a pause. A significant one. Finally, he asked, "Where *are* you?"

"I'm still at the house. I dealt with the car guy and came back in to set the alarm and your landline rang—and I know, I know. I had no right to answer it, but I did. And then, well, things just sort of seemed to take their own course. You know, conversation-wise."

"'Special friend' as in girlfriend?"

"Well, kind of, yes."

"You told Ma that we're a thing."

"Um. Not in so many words."

"Cami." He said it in a slightly pained way, but at least not in an angry way. "What are you up to?"

She went ahead and confessed. "I was just thinking that it's not a *bad* thing if your mom believes we're together, because if she thinks we're together she'll stop matchmaking you. I figure that if we convince her that you're with me, she'll leave you alone for at least six months." She paused, hoping he would jump in with reassurances.

Dead silence from him.

Finally, she offered sheepishly, "All righty, then. I'll just call her back and straighten things out with her."

"Absolutely not." He said that with zero hesitation. "You're in it now, Cami."

That didn't sound good. "In it, how?"

"You're going to my mother's with me tonight."

She brightened. "Excellent."

"You say that now, but you haven't met my mother."

Cami laughed. "I just talked to her. We had a nice little chat."

"Nobody has a nice little chat with my mother."

"Well, *I* did. And I'm very curious to meet her in person." And to see the mansion that had originally belonged to Willow's rival, Frank Bravo's first wife.

"I'm glad you're curious, because you *are* meeting her. We'll tell her tonight that she misunderstood about you and me."

For some unknown reason, Cami felt disappointed. "Fair enough."

"Okay, then—and I know you have a lot to do today." His voice had gentled. He sounded more like the Garrett she'd known on the mountain. "You think you can get it all finished in time to be home and ready at six forty-five?"

Home. She glanced around the beautiful kitchen and realized that she did feel very much at home there. "I'll be ready."

"Call me if you need anything."

"I will."

"And, Cami?"

"Yeah?"

"I know you were only trying to help me out." He said it low, with real affection. She felt warm all over. Someone spoke to him on his end. He said something back and then spoke to Cami again. "Gotta go."

"Bye…" Grinning, she ended the call.

"That was her?" Nell, Garrett's baby sister and business partner, popped a cherry Life Saver into her mouth and sucked on it thoughtfully. Nell wore dusty jeans, combat boots and a soft gray Bravo Construction T-shirt with the sleeves pushed up onto her shoulders. The shirt showed off the half sleeve of ink that covered her left arm from shoulder to elbow.

Garrett dropped the phone on his desk and chuckled to himself. "She let Ma think we're a thing."

"But you're not?" Nell gave him a sideways look.

"I told you, I like her a lot. She's going through some challenging stuff and I'm here to help her however I can. We're *friends*."

"The operative words being that you *like* her a *lot*." Nell tossed her long red hair.

"Don't even start with that crap. Please."

"Fine." Nell put up both hands. "Sorry. You like her a lot. But you don't *like* her a lot."

"You always were a pain in my ass."

"Go ahead. Be thickheaded. It kind of suits you."

"Brat."

She slouched back in her chair. "So. Will you take over with Deck?"

Declan McGrath had been Nell's high school boyfriend. He'd broken her heart back in the day. Now, more than a decade later, he'd decided he wanted another shot with her. Nell kept refusing to go out with him, but Deck wouldn't let it go. His latest move had been to approach her to build him a house.

Garrett shook his head. "The guy obviously wants to work with you, personally."

Nell leaned forward and braced her elbows on her knees. "Think of it this way. Deck is going to get someone to build him a new house. That someone should be us. And even though I don't want to deal with him *personally*, there's no reason that *you* can't. He's rolling in money now." Deck had done well for himself. He owned and ran Justice Creek Barrels. Apparently, there was big money in repurposing wine and whiskey barrels. Nell went on. "He's going to want the best and that's what we'll give him. Everybody wins. It's a no-brainer, big brother."

"He wants *you*. You hand him off to me, he's not going to be happy."

"Too bad. He wants a house. You can help him with that. The two of you get along fine."

"Nellie, come on. I bought the barrel tub up at the cabin from him. That doesn't exactly make Deck my best friend."

"Speaking of the cabin," Nell began way too casually. "Who held down the fort here while you were up on the mountain hiding from Ma? Why, I believe that might have been me, your long-suffering, hard-working sister and business partner."

Garrett gave up. "Point taken. I'll call Deck and set up a first consultation."

"You are my favorite brother."

"I know—well, aside from Carter and Quinn and James and Darius."

"Ha. When do I get to meet Cami? I have a feeling I'm going to love her."

Garrett had no doubt on that score. "She really is something. Gorgeous, definitely. But even better, she's so easy to be around and she's smart and funny. And tough, too, at heart. Nothing gets her down."

"So what you're saying is, when it comes to Cami, what's not to love?"

"Exactly."

"And I know you mean that in a purely friends-only kind of way."

He tried a scowl. "Get off my case, Nellie."

"I'm still not really clear on how you and Cami met…"

"It's a long story." He made a mental note to ask

Cami how much of that story she wanted shared. For now, he played it vague. "I think I'll let her tell it."

Nell gave him a wink. "You be sure to say hi to Ma for me tonight."

At the Broomtail County Justice Center, Cami asked for Garrett's brother-in-law, Sheriff Seth Yancy. The sheriff, a big guy with kind eyes and a confident manner, ushered her into his office and listened to her story.

He quizzed her about her black eye and the healing scratches on her face and arms and asked if they were all from the accident. When she confirmed that they were, he said he wanted to have a look at the scene before anyone disturbed it, just on the off chance they might get a lead on who ran her off the road. He promised he would call her and let her know when they'd "released the scene" so that she could arrange for a tow.

Her phone was ringing in her purse as she left the justice center. She checked the display.

It was Charles.

"Not talking to you right now," she muttered under her breath. Setting the phone to Silent Page, she put it away.

Then she headed for Central Street, stopping first at a stationery and art supply store, where she stocked up on sketch pads, colored pencils, pastels and several packages of colored paper. Art supplies soothed her soul. They also helped her brainstorm ideas. And she needed ideas for her future, because not only was she going to make her home in Justice Creek, she also planned to find herself a career that would include her love of drawing and art.

What career exactly? She had no clue. Sooner or later, though, she would figure it out.

After the stationery store, she wandered from one boutique to the next buying clothes, shoes, makeup and toiletries. It took hours. She could probably have returned to Denver and cleared out her closet at the condo in the same amount of time.

But she wasn't ready to face going back. Not yet. Plus, there was something hopeful and liberating about getting everything new. She felt grateful to have the money to do that, to buy brighter colors than she used to wear, to choose clothes in an easier, less structured style than before.

She found a lingerie store and bought a boatload of underwear, some filmy nighties she didn't really need and a couple of cute sleep shirts. It was a truly great moment to finally take off her wedding bustier and put on a comfortable bra for a change. A block from the lingerie store, she stuffed the bustier in a trash can and congratulated herself on the fact that she would never have to look it—let alone wear it—again.

By five, when she headed back to Garrett's, the Subaru was piled high with shopping bags and she'd decided that when she did go back to Denver to pack up her condo, she would donate all her designer clothes to Goodwill.

When Cami emerged from her bedroom in a little white dress printed with bright red cherries that clung to her curves, Garrett had one word for her.

"Wow."

She giggled in that happy way she had and twirled around. "I went shopping." Her blond hair was sleek and shiny to her shoulders and she wore red sandals with delicate high heels.

"I can't even tell you have a black eye."

"It's the magic of makeup, Garrett." She bent to scratch Munch behind the ears. "Hey, handsome. You be good while we're gone." Munch gave a happy whine in response. "You look very handsome, too." She nodded approvingly at his blue knit shirt and khaki pants.

It felt a little strange, he realized, to be taking her to his mother's. In fact, it felt a whole lot like a date.

But it wasn't. And they would clear that up with Ma when they got to the mansion.

Out in the garage, he led her to the Ferrari-red 1969 Mustang Grande he rarely drove. He'd decided on the Mustang because the Jeep was dusty and spattered with mud, not because he wanted to impress her or anything.

"Gorgeous old car," she said as she settled into the leather seat.

He explained that his older brother Carter customized cars for a living. "He fixed this one up just for me."

The ride to the Bravo mansion was a short one. Cami gave him a rundown of her visit with Seth at the justice center and all the stuff she'd bought that afternoon. "I know it's self-indulgent to buy everything new. But I did it anyway. A whole new wardrobe." She smoothed the skirt of her cherry-covered dress. "To start my whole new life." She gave him a glowing smile, and he felt great just being with her in her pretty dress, driving with the windows down on a warm summer evening.

He'd already pulled to a stop in the sweeping turn-around in front of his mother's ostentatious white house before he realized they hadn't agreed on what exactly she was willing to say about how she'd ended up on Moosejaw Mountain with him.

Not that they really needed to discuss it in advance. He decided to follow Cami's lead. It was her story. Let her tell it in her own way.

They went up the wide steps between the two pretentious white pillars. Estrella, the mansion's longtime housekeeper, pulled the door open before he even rang the bell. "Garrett. So good to see you."

"Come in, come in!" His mother, in a pale green silk dress, her slim arms spread wide, emerged from the living room off the entry hall. Estrella stepped back, and Willow grabbed him in a hug. "I'm so glad you're here," she said softly. Her perfume, some light yet exotic scent she had made specially in Paris, swam around him. The hug kind of bewildered him. Willow Bravo had never been much of a hugger. She must really be happy that he'd finally found a girlfriend. He almost felt bad to have to tell her the truth. "And you must be Cami." She reached for Cami.

"Mrs. Bravo."

"Willow," his mother corrected as she drew Cami close. "It is simply wonderful to meet you." The women pulled apart and beamed at each other.

"Garrett's told me so much about you," Cami said.

Willow smirked. "He's complained about me, hasn't he? Go ahead and admit it."

"Never," replied Cami with a mock-serious frown.

And then the two of them laughed together, like they shared some kind of tasty little secret that no man could ever understand.

"Drinks in the library." Willow swept out a hand. "This way."

They went through the formal living room into the room behind it, where carved, built-in shelves held rows of leather-bound, gold-tooled volumes. A giant fireplace dominated one wall and the center of the room held twin damask sofas, a scattering of silk-covered chairs, carved side tables and a large, inlaid coffee table. Willow gestured at one of the sofas. Garrett sat down and Cami sat next to him, a lot closer than she really needed to on such a big couch.

But really, Garrett didn't mind her sitting close. She looked adorable in that dress—adorable and happy. That made him happy, too. And she smelled like sunshine and vanilla and some flower he couldn't quite recall the name of. Frangipani, maybe? Jasmine?

No, he didn't mind her sitting close in the least—though he did kind of worry it would reinforce his mother's incorrect assumptions about their relationship.

Willow went to the ornate drink cart between two of the chairs. "Martini?" He would have preferred whiskey or ice-cold vodka, straight, but his mother loved martinis and served them up every chance she got.

"Yes, please!" Cami replied with great enthusiasm. "Good and dirty, if you don't mind. I love the taste of olives. Just can't help myself."

"Dirty, it is," Willow replied, sounding downright gleeful. His mother. Gleeful. Would the weirdness never cease? "Garrett?"

"Sure, Ma. Thanks."

Willow expertly mixed their drinks, skipping the vermouth for Cami's and using olive juice instead.

"And I would like to propose a toast." Willow raised her glass high. "To love and happiness for both of you. I'm so pleased that you've found each other."

Garrett opened his mouth to explain that he and Cami were strictly in the friend zone, but Cami gave him a fond little bump with her shoulder and piped right up with, "To love and happiness." She clicked her glass with Garrett's first and then with Willow's. And she looked so sweet and pleased with the situation, it seemed just plain mean-spirited to argue the point now.

So he went ahead and let his mother tap her glass against his, figuring he might as well be sociable and just finish the toast. He could find another opportunity to correct the misunderstanding about him and Cami.

Garrett waited for the right moment.

But somehow, another opportunity never came. They finished their drinks, his mother rambling on about her latest trip. She'd gone to Sweden. Cami had been to Sweden twice, as it turned out. She said how much she loved the botanical gardens in Gothenburg and the Icehotel—an actual hotel made of ice—in some city with a name he'd never heard before.

When they sat down to dinner, Willow asked Cami about her family and her work. Cami managed to tell his mother the truth about growing up in Denver and the Lockwood vitamin empire without revealing that she'd recently left her groom at the altar or how, specifically, she and Garrett had met.

Garrett listened to the women laughing and chattering away and realized he was having a really good time—the most fun he'd ever had at the stuffy Bravo mansion, that was for sure. And it was all because of Cami, who had somehow turned his usually distant mother into someone warm and sociable.

He did snap to attention, though, when Cami said, "You know how these things go, Willow. Garrett and I found each other up on the mountain, and it was so special, right from the beginning, from the first moment our eyes met. We've been virtually inseparable ever since."

Inseparable? Okay, maybe they hadn't been apart until today, but still. She was definitely carrying the whole thing too far. He really did need to call a halt to this silly game before it got way out of hand.

So he opened his mouth and flatly announced, "Wait a minute. I just want to clarify. Cami's exaggerating. We are not dating. She is not my 'special' friend."

Chapter Four

Cami gasped. Willow blinked and gaped at Garrett.

Okay, maybe that had been a little abrupt. But it couldn't be helped. He needed to make the truth of their situation perfectly clear before his mother got too invested in the idea that he and Cami were a couple.

Didn't he?

And then Cami reached over and put her soft little hand over his. "Wow. That is so harsh. Garrett, you're such a mess."

Now he was the one gaping. He ought to yank his hand out from under hers and tell her to cut it the hell out.

But he didn't. Her hand felt so good touching his. And he just sat there and stared at her and wondered how a woman could be so completely impossible and so downright adorable, both at the same time.

She turned to Willow. "Clearly, he has a thousand emotional issues."

"Yes," said Willow somberly. "I'm afraid that he does. I don't know if he's told you how it was for him—for all five of my children—growing up?"

"Well, he did mention something about his half siblings and your, um, husband's first wife. And… all that."

"So then, you do understand? It was a difficult time and all the children were affected. And yes, I blame myself. Rightfully so."

"Well, but it's in the past, isn't it?" Cami asked gently.

"Yes, but I—"

"And Garrett says all nine of your husband's children get along great now. They've all moved on. You just have to forgive yourself, Willow. *You* have to move on."

"I'm trying."

"I'm so glad." Cami's full lips bloomed in a gorgeous smile. Then she frowned. "As for Garrett, well, I realize I've got a big job ahead of me, getting him to open up and give his heart freely. One minute he loves me, the next I'm 'not his special friend.' Sometimes I kind of wonder why I try. But love is like that, right? You just keep working, keep plugging away. When you love someone, what else can you do?"

Willow knocked back a big gulp of the white wine Estrella had served with the trout almondine and nodded in bemused agreement. "Yes. I see that." She echoed Cami softly, "What else can you do?"

With a final, gentle pat, Cami let Garrett's hand

go. "It's all right, sweetheart." Her eyes, of that mesmerizing otherworldly blue, held his. "I understand."

Garrett opened his mouth to ask her if she had lost her ever-loving mind.

And then he just couldn't do that.

She was trying to help him. And really, why was he making such a big deal of this? What could it hurt?

If Ma wanted to believe he and Cami were a thing and Cami wanted to play the role of devoted girlfriend, well, why the hell not?

It was almost ten, the night clear and warm, when they got in the car and headed back down the curving driveway away from the mansion. Garrett didn't say anything during the short drive home.

Cami leaned her head back against the seat rest and really hoped he wasn't furious with her.

At his house, she set her purse on the kitchen table and bent to greet Munchy, who gave her a bunch of doggy kisses and then turned to get some love from Garrett, too. He knelt to ruffle the dog's fur.

Cami gathered her courage and asked, "Are you mad at me for lying to your mother and making her think we're in love?"

He held her gaze over the wiggling body of the dog between them. "It did kind of freak me out at first."

A nervous laugh escaped her. "I noticed that."

"But I got over it."

She couldn't resist teasing him. "For a minute there, I was sure you were going to tell your mom I was crazy and should probably seek professional help."

Munchy's claws tapped the wood floor as he trotted to his water bowl to lap up a drink. Garrett stood and she did, too. "You were so determined."

"I know I should have taken the hint when you tried to put the brakes on."

There was definitely the ghost of a smile on his beautiful mouth. "But instead, you went all in with it." When the dog padded to the glass door and sat down, Garrett opened it for him. Munch slipped out.

She confessed, "I think I went *too* far with that stuff about how messed up you are. Sorry."

"Hey. You were playing it for all you were worth. And Ma wanted to believe you so badly. I didn't have the heart to keep fighting you both."

Cami slipped off her red sandals. The cool wood floor felt good against her bare feet. "I'm just glad you're not angry with me."

"I'm not." His voice was low and a little bit rough and the two of them were just standing there, staring at each other.

Good gravy, he was hot, with those melty amber eyes, those fine, broad shoulders. And that tender heart of his that he didn't even realize was so good, so true.

Was she falling for him?

Or was it only that Garrett and this bold, beautiful new life where she was finally becoming her real self were somehow intertwined for her? She had found him on the mountain and she'd loved every minute of her life since then—even the crappy ones, like almost losing Munchy to an angry bear and having to deal with her parents and Charles.

He said, "Plus…"

"Yeah?"

"Well, you were right that if she thinks we're together, she'll get off my case for a while. I wouldn't mind that in the least."

A lightness stole through Cami. "Good. I know it's not much, but it's nice to be able to tell myself that *I'm* finally doing something for *you*. And I've been thinking. Um, you mentioned my staying here?"

"The offer's still open."

"I'm glad. Because I want to stay here with you." At his slow, flirty grin, she shook her red sandals at him. "You are such a teaser. I mean, as a roomie. Of course I'll pay rent. You should think it over."

"Forget the rent."

"But, Garrett—"

"And I don't need to think it over. I want you to stay for as long as you need a place. And not because your staying helps me catch a break from Ma, either, though I've decided not to complain if it does. But the real deal is, I kind of hate to see you go." Oh, she did like the sound of that. "Life's a lot more interesting with you around."

Was he flirting with her? And was she a fool to hope so?

He opened the glass door again and Munch came back in. "Like I said, the offer's open. It's up to you." Munch fell into step behind him as he headed for the living room. "'Night, Cami."

"'Night…" He disappeared on his way to the stairs in the front hall.

She almost felt sad to see him go.

Garrett was sound asleep when he heard a soft tap on his bedroom door. "Garrett?" It was Cami's voice.

"Huh?" He came wide awake suddenly and squinted at the bedside clock—11:34.

"Garrett?" More tapping. Munch was already over there, whining and wagging his tail.

"Give me a minute!" He turned on the lamp and then grabbed the sweats he'd thrown across the bench at the foot of the bed.

When he opened the door, she looked up at him through anxious eyes. "Sorry." She wore a giant pink T-shirt with a cupcake printed on the front. And she must have noticed he was staring at the sparkly sprinkles in the frosting—or more specifically, at the soft curves of her braless breasts underneath. She looked down at the breasts in question. "New sleep shirt. I could never resist a great big cupcake, especially one with sprinkles."

"Cute," he said. Because it was—and so was she. And he was *not* thinking about her breasts, which were just right, round and full and...

Uh-uh. Not going there. No way. She seemed sad or worried about something. She'd probably come to him for comfort. The last thing she needed was to catch him sporting wood.

She patted Munch on the head. "I woke you up."

"It's okay."

"No, it's not. You're never going to want me for a roomie if I won't even let you sleep at night."

He leaned against the door frame. "Did you wake me up to say you're sorry for waking me up?"

She seemed to consider his silly question, but then she said, "I miss the cabin. I know that's crazy. I wasn't there for all that long. But I miss it anyway. I miss the way we would talk at night after you turned off the light."

He couldn't figure out her mood exactly. But something was bugging her. "You need to talk now?"

She caught her lower lip between her pretty white teeth—and nodded.

He took her hand, loving the way her cool fingers curled trustingly in his. She didn't object as he pulled her into the room and led her to the far side of the bed.

"What a beautiful bed." She touched the headboard, running her fingers along the weathered wood.

"It's repurposed, made of wood from old barns. Lie down." She jumped right up and stretched out on top of the covers. He got the extra blanket and settled it over her, then went back around and got in on his side. Munch joined them, curling up at their feet. Garrett turned out the light and adjusted his pillow under his head. "Comfy?"

He heard a soft sigh from her side of the bed. "Very."

"Now, talk."

"I feel kind of bad bothering you with this."

"Talk."

She came out with it then. "It's Charles."

"What did that bonehead do now?"

"He just keeps calling. And texting. I turned my phone down in the afternoon and ignored him. And then I powered it off when we went to your mother's. When I turned it back on an hour ago, I had three new calls and four texts from him. I've gotten zero calls from my parents, which leads me to believe my father has ordered Charles to get busy and get me back in line. Charles does what Quentin Lockwood tells him to do and that means he's not going to back off until I agree to see him."

Garrett hadn't even met the guy, but he already wanted to punch Charles's lights out. He didn't think much of her father, either. "You really believe that a face-to-face with your ex-groom is going make a difference?"

"I don't know. Not for sure. But I guess I kind of feel I owe it to him. I should have broken it off with him in person, but I knew if I did, the chances of making my escape would not be good."

"Because the guy is so damn convincing?"

"No. Because Charles would have run straight to my father and my father would have found a way to keep me from going. I can't tell you how many times my father has managed to stop me from striking out on my own, how many times I've run away and then screwed up and ended up right back where I never wanted to be. I'm not screwing up this time. I'm free and I'm staying free."

"I believe you," he said with real admiration. "What I can't believe is that you didn't get out on your own long before now."

"See? That's another thing I like about you. You think I'm strong and tough and ready for anything."

"Because you are—and what do you mean, you screwed up in the past?"

"I just mean that something would always happen and I would have to go back to Denver and the over-protective bosom of my family. I told you about that time after college, when that drunk driver crashed into me and I ended up in a coma?"

"You did. You also mentioned it wasn't the first time."

"And it wasn't. The first time, I was ten."

"Okay. That's a little young to strike out on your own."

"You're right. But I did it anyway. And I only got lost and ended up huddled in a shed in a snowstorm for two days, afraid I would die."

"My God."

Her hand brushed his shoulder, a quick pat of reassurance, and then it was gone. "Don't worry. I got through it. The man who owned the shed found me. His wife gave me some hot soup and called the police. A lady from child protective services came and took me back to my parents. They grounded me for months and made me get counseling."

"Did *they* get counseling?"

"Are you kidding? *I'm* the one with problems, remember?"

"They could have made a little effort to understand what was bothering you."

"Hmm. I think they really believe that they *have* made the effort to understand me. And what they understand is that *I'm* the one who's making the trouble, that instead of facing my issues, I run away."

"Because they won't listen to you and work with you to help you have the kind of life that suits you."

She laughed. The sound made his chest feel tight in a really satisfying way. "I love the way you think, Garrett."

He grunted, because now his throat felt a little tight, too. "So what happened next?"

"Well, in high school, I fell for a bad boy. Robbie

Rodriquez worked at Taco Bell. I went in for a chili verde burrito and got lost in his big brown eyes. We ran away together. But then it turned out that Robbie wasn't so very bad, after all. A couple of days on the road and he started worrying about his family. He said he couldn't do it, couldn't just walk away from everyone who loved him."

Garrett laced his hands behind his head and stared up at the shadowed ceiling. "So you went back to Denver."

"We did. My father was furious and my mother was worried sick. I felt just awful. I got more therapy. My counselor was patient and understanding and helped me to see that running away wasn't the solution."

Given all that she'd told him, Garrett wasn't sure he agreed with her therapist. Not in her particular case, anyway. "What *was* the solution?"

She chuckled and poked him with her elbow. "That's the problem. I don't think there is a solution when it comes to my father. Except to get away from him and stay away long enough that he finally has to accept that this is my life and I'm the one who gets to choose how to live it."

"Sounds like a plan to me."

"See?" She scooted closer. He smelled her scent of vanilla and tropical flowers. And then he felt her soft lips brush his cheek. She was back on her own side of the bed before he could do anything stupid— like grab her close and hold on tight. "That's why I need to be with you right now," she said. "Because you *get* me, Garrett. You get me in a way that no one else ever has. You make me strong."

His throat still felt weirdly tight. He had to speak around the irritating obstruction. "You *are* strong." It came out rough with emotion he didn't want to examine.

And she laughed. He didn't think he'd ever get enough of hearing her laugh. "See? That. What you said right there? That's what I'm talkin' about."

A silence descended, a companionable one. It went on for a while. It felt so good, just lying here beside her. He stared at the ceiling. His eyelids were growing heavy.

In a minute, he'd be falling asleep. And they had yet to settle the question of what she should do about Charles.

He blinked a few times to wake himself up. "So… about Charles. Are you going to meet with him?"

"Mmm-hmm. I'm thinking tomorrow. You know, get it over with. Probably someplace public."

That alarmed him a little. "Why? Are you afraid of him?"

"Not afraid, just…" She seemed to have trouble finding the right word.

He felt for her hand. When he had it, he twined their fingers together. "I'm listening. Tell me."

"Charles is always so sure he's right. He's like my father that way. Relentless in getting what he wants."

"You think he'll bully you into going back to him?"

"I'm pretty sure he's going to try. That's why I plan to meet him at a restaurant or something, someplace where he'll be reluctant to make a scene."

"I don't get the guy's reasoning. Even if he talked you into coming back, what kind of life would you have together if one of you just wants to get away?"

She squeezed his hand a little tighter. "It's not really me that he wants. It's WellWay. Marrying the boss's daughter is a means to seal that deal up tight."

"Wait a minute. You're saying he doesn't even love you?"

"You sound angry." She eased her hand free of his.

He had to resist the urge to grab it back. "I'm sorry. But everything you've told me about this guy just pisses me off."

"It's complicated. I mean, I'm pretty sure he *thinks* he loves me, that he *tells* himself he loves me. I'm also positive he loves WellWay more. And he's been really good for the company. He's ambitious, creative, hardworking and smart. When my father retires, Charles *should* be the one to step up and run the company."

"So then, there's the solution. You don't have to marry Charles in order for him to end up as CEO of the company he loves so damn much."

"That's not how my father sees it. It's a family company and I'm his only child. He wants me to take over from him eventually. If I marry Charles, we can take it over together. I think that's the optimum outcome as far as my dad is concerned. I marry Charles and that locks me in to living the life my father wants for me, plus it makes Charles truly one of the family. He'll be there to make sure I stay in line after my parents are gone."

"*Stay in line?* That's just scary, Cami. I'm glad you escaped."

She let out a low, sweet chuckle. "You have no idea how happy it makes me that you understand how I feel, what I need."

"But you still think you have to meet with Charles—and what is his last name, anyway?"

"Ashby. Charles Ashby. And yeah. I think I do. For the sake of closure, you know?"

"Wasn't it closure enough that you left him at the altar?"

"Spoken like a guy. Garrett, closure doesn't work like that."

"Why? Because it's not closure if you don't talk it to death?"

She softly sighed. "Eventually, I have to go see my parents, too, and try to make peace with them. But one big helping of awfulness at a time. Charles first."

"Tell him you'll meet him here at the house. I'll be here when you do. If he gives you any crap, Munch and I will come running."

She was quiet for the longest time. He wondered if she'd dropped off to sleep.

But then she confessed glumly, "I came in here hoping you'd say that. Now I'm thinking I'm a manipulative jerk to get you involved in this."

"You're not a jerk. And you didn't manipulate me. I volunteered. In fact, I volunteered back at lunchtime, remember? I said if you were going to meet with him, meet with him here."

"I know, but—"

"Stop arguing. Tell me you'll talk to him here at the house."

Another silence. Then, softly, "I will."

"Now, get some sleep." He half expected her to jump up and run off back to her room.

But all she said was, "All right, then. 'Night."

* * *

In the morning when he woke up, she was still there beside him in bed, sound asleep, looking sweet as an angel—if an angel can have a black eye.

Very carefully, so as not to wake her yet, he got up on an elbow and stared at her sleeping face, thinking that he was kind of crazy about her.

How did that happen?

He decided that how didn't matter. He liked her. A lot.

It didn't have to be a big freaking deal.

She opened her eyes and looked straight at him. "Huh? What'd I do?"

"Nothing." He fell back to his own pillow and put his arm across his face before admitting out of the corner of his mouth, "I was just watching you sleep, that's all."

He felt the bed shift as she levered up and leaned over him. "Like in a pervy way?"

He groaned. "Possibly." And then he distinctly heard her snicker. He lowered his arm enough to look at her above him as she chortled away. "That does it. If you're just going to laugh at me, I'm never perving on you again." That only made her laugh harder. She fell back to her own pillow. He muttered, "I suppose it is kind of funny…"

Okay, not *that* funny. But he couldn't help grinning. He felt good—good about everything, for some unknown reason. He started laughing, too.

For two or three minutes, they just lay there in bed, staring at the ceiling and laughing together.

Then Munch, who was already at the bedroom door waiting to go outside, gave an extraloud whine.

They got up together and let him out.

* * *

Cami called Ashby after breakfast, while they were still at the table having second cups of coffee.

The guy was a douche, no doubt about it. Garrett couldn't hear the other end of the conversation. But Cami hardly got more than a couple of words out before Ashby would interrupt her. Finally, she said she would see him that evening. He seemed to be insisting he was coming right now.

She held firm. "Seven tonight. Or tomorrow night, if that works better for you."

He must have agreed. She rattled off Garrett's address.

Ashby said something else.

And Cami started to argue again. "No, Charles. I told you—" She pulled the phone away from her ear and glared at it.

Garrett set down his mug. "What happened?"

"I do not *believe* that man. He said he'll be here in an hour and a half. And then he hung up." Her sweet mouth trembled a little and two spots of hectic color rode high on her cheeks.

"Hey." He got up and went around to her, pulled her up into his arms and stroked a hand down her hair—because he wanted to, because his touch seemed to soothe her and he really liked touching her. Then he took that fairy princess face between his hands and held her gaze. "Look at it this way. It's better to get it over with. In a couple of hours, you'll be done with him."

She stared up at him anxiously. "I'll bet you need to get to work, huh?"

"No way am I leaving you here alone for this. I'll hang around just in case you need backup."

"Now I'm messing up your workday."

He smoothed her hair behind her ear. "No, you're not. I've got lunch with a prospective client at one. Nothing important until then."

Garrett managed to convince her to let him answer the door, so that Ashby would know from the get-go that she wasn't alone, that she had someone to stand up for her if it came to that.

Ashby, who was tall, with blond hair and cool blue eyes, didn't waste a second being friendly. "Who are you?" he demanded when Garrett pulled back the door.

"I live here."

"What?" The guy was good-looking, Garrett supposed. If you liked them really lean with pointy, over-bred features. And that lightweight gray suit he was wearing looked like Armani. "Where's Camilla?"

"I'm right here," Cami said from back near the stairs. Munch, at her feet, gave a low, warning growl. "Shh, Munchy," she soothed. "Everything's okay." Then she spoke to Ashby. "Come in, Charles."

Garrett was blocking the door, but he didn't move. He seriously did not like the guy. He and Ashby spent several seconds just glaring at each other.

"Garrett," Cami said, more strongly. "Please."

Reluctantly, he moved aside and gestured the other man in.

"Camilla, who is this man?" Ashby demanded once he'd cleared the threshold. "Why are you here?"

"Mind your manners, Ashby," Garrett warned. "Or I'll mind them for you."

Ashby turned on him. "Who *are* you? I don't know you."

Before Garrett could put the pretentious ass in his place, Cami said, "Charles, this is my friend Garrett. Let's go on in the kitchen." She turned and headed through the living room, Munch at her heels. With a last glare at Garrett, Ashby followed. Garrett took up the rear.

"Sit down, Charles." Cami gestured at the table. "Coffee?"

Charles did not sit. "No coffee." He sent another chilly glance at Garrett. "I want to talk to you alone. I think you owe me that."

Munch growled again. Garrett was about to inform the arrogant idiot that Cami didn't owe him squat.

But she caught his eye first. "It's okay. I do need speak with him in private."

Garrett didn't think she needed any such thing. But it was her fight. He got that. "Fair enough." He marched to the door on the other side of the island, the one to the hallway that led to the laundry room.

Ashby muttered something under his breath and Munch growled again.

"Hush, now," Cami soothed the dog. And then she looked at Garrett again. "I think you'd better take Munchy with you."

Garrett clicked his tongue. "Munch. Come." With one more watch-yourself growl for good measure, Munch followed him out. Garrett closed the door behind them.

Then, feeling no shame whatsoever, he pressed his ear to the door.

* * *

Cami waited until she heard Garrett shut the kitchen door before trying to settle Charles down a little. "Come on, Charles. Have a seat and we'll talk."

Charles shot his cuffs and stood straighter. "I'll stand. What's happened to your eye? Did that guy—?"

"Please. Garrett would never lay a finger on me."

"But if he's—"

"I had a little accident, that's all. I wrecked the Beemer."

"What in the...? How could you?"

"Actually, the accident wasn't my fault."

"You have a bruise on your chin. Have you been to a doctor? I don't believe this. What if you have internal injuries? Are you sure you don't need—"

"I'm perfectly fine. You really need to calm down a little, Charles."

"Calm down? *I* should calm down? I don't even know how to start with you, Camilla. You've been in a *car* accident?"

She waved a hand. "Like that hasn't happened before. I told you, I'm fine. Will you please let it go?"

"You left me at the church. I can't believe you would humiliate me that way. And now you've moved in with some strange guy in this nowhere little tourist town? You've always been a little too quirky and unusual for your own good, but as of this moment, I'm starting to think you've gone stark-raving nuts." He finally paused for a breath.

And she asked mildly, "Well, then, I guess it's all worked out for the best, hasn't it?"

"The best? What are you talking about?"

"Charles. It was a bad idea, you and me getting

married. I never should have said yes in the first place and I apologize for not ending it in a more considerate way. But it's done now and we can both move on."

He made a sputtering sound. "Move on? We're not moving on. Whatever gave you that idea?"

"Well, given that I ran out on our wedding and disappeared for several days without a word, it ought to be pretty clear to you by now that what we had wasn't working for me."

"Clear? What are you saying? None of that matters."

"Charles. Wake up. It matters."

"It does not. Of course we're going to work this out. Of course I will somehow learn to forgive you. We'll return home today. The license is still good and I've spoken with the priest. We can be married this afternoon and go on as we should have on Saturday—minus the reception, with the honeymoon slightly shortened." He raked his fingers through his pale blond hair. "So get whatever things you have here and I'll take you home now."

Cami knew she wasn't getting through to him, but she refused to become discouraged. She tried again. "Stop. Think. You have to know it would be a disaster. We'd only end up divorced."

"That's not true."

"You need to face facts here. I don't love you, Charles. And you don't love me, either."

He winced. It was only the slightest tightening around his mouth and eyes, but Cami saw it. And then he insisted woodenly, "Of course I love you."

"No, you don't. You love WellWay and you want to be president and CEO someday."

He looked pained. And she knew why. Because he did want to be president. He wanted it more than anything—even if he had to marry Quentin Lockwood's wayward daughter to get there. He said wearily, "We'll run the company together."

"No. *You* will run the company whether I'm there or not. And you deserve to run the company when my father retires. You don't need to marry the boss's daughter to make that happen."

"No, I… Cami, you know we're perfect for each other."

"That's not true."

"Of course it's true. You know that, in the end, this is all going to work out."

"Yes, it *is* going to work out. But not in the way you keep insisting. It's over between us, Charles. I never should have agreed to marry you and I'm not going to Denver with you today. I'm not going to Denver at all. Not for a while, anyway."

"You don't mean that."

"And you need to stop telling me what I think and feel. Listen, I was weak. You kept asking and, well, you know my father. He kept pushing. I finally gave in. But that's all it was. Just another sad surrender to my father's relentless push to run my life. We are not a good match. We would make each other miserable. Face it. Please. You don't love me, Charles."

"Yes, I do."

"No, you don't. If you did, I wouldn't have caught you kissing your secretary the day before our wedding."

Chapter Five

Garrett, his ear pressed to the other side of the kitchen door, could hardly believe what he'd just heard.

The bastard had *cheated* on her? Why hadn't she said so? This wasn't right. The argument on the other side of the door shouldn't even be happening. Ashby didn't deserve any damn closure if he'd been fooling around behind her back.

Garrett threw the door wide and headed for Ashby, Munch at his heels.

Cami whirled and put her hand out. "Garrett, don't."

"Do you *mind*?" Ashby demanded from the far side of the table. "This is a private conversation."

Munch gave a long, low growl and Garrett took another step toward the cheating SOB Cami almost married.

But then she reached out and grabbed his arm. "I mean it, Garrett. No."

"But he cheat—"

"Please." Her eyes were so soft, her tone way too anxious. "This is for me to handle." She moved in closer and pressed her hand to his chest. He smelled her sweet perfume, wanted to grab her fingers, pull her behind him and face that rich-boy punk across the table for her.

But those beautiful blue eyes told him no.

Beside him, Munch let out another growl. "Come on, boy." Garrett bent enough to get the dog by his collar and led him back into the hallway, pulling the door closed behind him again.

Cami watched the door close on Garrett's face and realized she was totally falling for him. He was a true friend.

And more. So much more. He was everything she'd begun to think she'd never find in a guy. Funny and helpful, bighearted and smart. Not to mention, way hot.

But how she felt about Garrett wasn't the issue right now.

Right now, she needed to finish this sad thing with Charles.

She turned on her heel and went back to face him across the table. "All right." She even managed a smile. "Where were we?"

His lip curled downward, a frown that was also partly a sneer. "Get your things. We are leaving."

A shiver raced up her spine as she realized how much he sounded like her father. Thank God she hadn't married him. "No, Charles. *I'm* not leaving. Yes, I admit that I've been a coward. But not anymore. If I had loved you, walking in on you kissing someone else would have devastated me, but all I felt was a kind of numb disbelief that I was marrying you the next day and we didn't even love each other."

"Of course I love you," Charles said automatically. But he actually looked a little ashamed. "And as for that little incident with Tricia, you...didn't say anything at the time."

"Except for *excuse me*, you mean?" She'd been pretty stunned. "I didn't know what to say. So I just shut the door and left."

"I assumed you understood that it was nothing."

"Well, you assumed wrong."

"I swear to you, Camilla. It was only that one kiss. I don't know what I was thinking. Tricia is flirtatious, yes. But she's an excellent assistant and we've always kept it strictly business."

"Except for the flirting and the kissing, you mean?"

Charles raked a hand back over his hair. "Don't be sarcastic."

"Sorry, but a little sarcasm seems totally appropriate about now."

"What did you expect me to do? You would never let me near you."

Because we didn't love each other. "You felt deprived. Is that what you're saying?"

"You know I did."

"So you got involved with Tricia."

"No. Of course not. That's not what I said."

She actually almost felt sorry for him. "Charles. You were as trapped as I was. Admit it. Move on."

He drew his shoulders back, as though by standing straighter he could somehow put himself in the right. "What I'm trying to tell you is that I have never touched Tricia before or since."

She really did wish she could get through to him. "But, Charles, don't you see? If it was true love between us, you never would have touched Tricia at all."

"No. Now, that's just not so. Do you have to romanticize *everything*? I did love you—I *do* love you. And you are twisting my words. I am saying that my kissing Tricia was only one of those silly things that happen now and then. Eventually, you will stop being so ridiculously naive and realize that a meaningless kiss is nothing to get all upset about."

"Charles." She gave him a long look of great patience. "When a woman catches her fiancé kissing another woman, it is definitely something for her to get upset about—and before you start in with your denials again, I want you to understand that I do see my own part in this."

"Well, that's something at least. If you hadn't been so cold, I never would have—"

"Charles. Forget Tricia. And anyone else you fooled around with while we were engaged."

"I never—"

"Oh, please. When are you going to face that you were as unhappy with me as I was with you?"

"What? No. Of course I wasn't unhappy. How can you say that? There you go being difficult again."

"Here I go telling the truth. Again. And you know it, too. I should never have agreed to marry you. And when I finally woke up and admitted to myself that it wasn't going to work, I should have done a better job of calling it off. But still, ending it was the right thing to do and you should be grateful that I came to my senses and ran before we actually got married and made everything worse."

"Grateful?" he huffed in outrage. "I should be *grateful…*"

"Yes, you should."

"Well, I am not grateful. And this conversation is not going anywhere. I've promised your father I will bring you back today and, one way or another, that is exactly what I intend to do."

"Oh, now." She shook her head. "See? There it is. That is the real reason you're here and we both know it. You're here because my father sent you."

He didn't even bother to deny it. "We are going home now."

She took his ring from her pocket. "*I'm* going nowhere. Here's your ring." She held it up for him. "Take it and leave, please."

Fast as a striking snake, as she bent to set the ring on the table, he whipped out a hand and grabbed her wrist. "We're leaving together. Now." His grip was hard, punishing. She tried to jerk away, but he didn't release her. "Let's go."

She knew a flash of actual terror. And then she steeled herself. "Let go of me, Charles."

"We're out of here." He stepped clear of the table and yanked her toward him.

"No. Let me go!"

At her cry, the kitchen door burst open behind her, hitting the wall with a loud bang. Cami whipped her head toward the sound as a whirlwind of angry dog and furious man burst out. Munch and Garrett came flying toward her.

Charles let her go and jumped back, giving a yelp of fear as Munch latched on to the hem of his pant leg. The dog growled and the fabric tore.

"Munch!" Garrett commanded. "Sit!"

With one last, low growl, Munch released Charles's pricey pant leg and dropped to his haunches.

"Get the hell out," said Garrett.

Charles tugged on the sides of his jacket. "Your dog has destroyed a good pair of pants."

"Hang around," suggested Garrett, way too quietly, "and see what *I* destroy."

Cami breathed a careful sigh of relief as Charles swiped the ring off the table. "All right, Camilla, have it your way. We are through."

"Oh, yes, we are," she agreed with enthusiasm, catching hold of Munchy's collar before he got any more overly protective ideas.

"Out." Garrett took another step toward Charles.

"Don't you come near me." Charles backed toward the living room. Garrett followed, step for step, herding him toward the front door. "You know this isn't the end of it." Charles looked past Garrett at Cami as he continued moving backward. "You might be rid of me, because I'm done with you. But your father won't put up with this."

Cami refused to waver. "When you report to him, tell him I don't want to see him until I'm *ready* to see him and he'd better not turn up here uninvited."

Before Charles could reply, Garrett herded him out of sight. It was just as well, Cami decided as she heard the front door open and shut. She held on to

Munchy until Charles's Maserati started up outside. He peeled rubber pulling out.

"Show-off," Cami muttered to herself.

Garrett reappeared from the front hall. At her side, Munch gave a happy whine at the sight of his master.

"He's gone," Garrett said.

Her heart welling with happiness, she watched him approach. She'd faced down Charles and never wavered. And when things got out of hand, Garrett had been there to make it right.

With a glad cry, she threw herself against his broad, strong chest. His big arms went around her, banding tight. She pressed her cheek to his hard shoulder, breathed in his scent of pine and leather. He made her world feel safe and right.

"You okay?" His lips brushed the crown of her head. She felt his warm breath ruffle her hair.

And she looked up. His beautiful caramel eyes were waiting.

Did she speak his name? Or did she only hear it echo inside her with every hopeful beat of her hungry heart?

"Cami." There was an entire conversation just in the way that he whispered her name.

"Garrett." She said it out loud that time.

He made a low sound, like a question.

And she slipped her hand up his chest, over the thick, muscled curve of his shoulder, until she could clasp the nape of his neck. "Yes. Oh, yes…"

He lowered his mouth and she lifted up.

His warm, soft lips covered hers. She gave a happy cry and surged even closer. He tasted of coffee with a dollop of cream, of nights on the mountain and all the wonder and wild beauty that made up her new life. The life she'd always wanted, the life that used to seem so far away, moving ever farther out of reach.

But not anymore.

She pressed even closer, felt the evidence that he really, truly did want her.

And, oh, she wanted him, too. Wanted his kisses and his hands all over her, wanted him to scoop her up and carry her to his bedroom, where they could share a whole lot more than this perfect, tender kiss.

She wanted it all with him, for the very first time.

How strange life was. How many times had she puzzled over what, exactly, she was waiting for when it came to having sex?

Well, it all made sense now. She had waited for Garrett. He was always meant to be her first.

He lifted his head. She saw desire in his eyes. And hesitation, too. "I shouldn't—"

She stopped his words with her fingers to his lips. "Shh." *Don't ruin it. Just let it be.*

And he did. He let it be.

She said, "Somehow, I'm always thanking you." It came out in a whisper, fervent. Grateful. Overflowing with emotions she thought it safer not to name.

Yet.

He touched her chin, rubbed his rough thumb in a slow caress down the side of her cheek. "He's gone. I really don't think he'll be back."

"He was going to drag me out of here."

"But he didn't."

"Because of you."

One corner of that gorgeous, oh-so-kissable mouth of his kicked up. "Don't forget Munch, the wonder dog." At their feet, the dog in question thumped his tail against the floor.

"Never, ever could I forget Munchy."

"And you didn't tell me that Ashby was a cheater." He said it in a chiding way.

She combed the short hair at his temples with her fingers, because it felt good. Because he let her. "Charles kissing his secretary really wasn't the issue."

His eyes darkened. "It's exactly the issue. If a guy cheats, he doesn't deserve an explanation as to why a woman is done with him—and don't come back with how he didn't have sex with her. If he kissed her, you just don't know what else he was up to."

"But, Garrett, it was a good thing, the *best* thing, that I saw him kissing Tricia. It woke me up, you know? Made me finally admit that it was almost too late and I had to get out of there."

"Still. A cheater's a cheater. My dad cheated on his first wife with my mother. None of us ever completely forgave him for that. Or forgave my mother, for that matter."

"You said they're all past that."

"Okay, yeah. You're right. We do forgive. But we don't forget. We remember how their cheating hurt us, all of us. We Bravos—my generation, anyway—we don't cheat. Ever. And you should have told me what Ashby did."

"I guess I felt kind of sorry for him." At Garrett's snort of outrage, she made a low, soothing sound and pressed her hand against his cheek, just for a moment, just to watch the heat flare in those amber eyes. "Charles was my friend when we were kids. His dad and my dad were like brothers. Then his dad had some money problems and Charles had to take out serious loans just to get his education. WellWay is everything to him. It's his ticket back to the good life. He's as trapped as I ever was—more so, really. He's got no nest egg to count on if he walks away."

"Sorry. I'm not feeling any sympathy for the guy." He took a swatch of her hair and rubbed it between his fingers, tipping his head to the side in a thoughtful sort of way. "And we should talk about what just happened." He meant the kiss. She could see it in his eyes.

"Uh-uh." She tried to press her fingertips to his lips again.

But he caught them. "Cami, I kissed you."

"And I kissed you back. I liked it. A lot."

"So did I. But that's not what matters."

"Garrett. It is exactly what matters."

"You really are too tempting, you know that?" He brought her captured fingers close then and brushed his warm lips against them.

Pleasure shivered through her. "All I'm saying is don't you dare try to talk yourself out of kissing me again."

"It's what you want?" His eyes were almost golden now. "More kisses from me?"

I want it all from you. Everything. At last. "More kisses. Yes."

"More kisses will take us beyond the friend zone." It was a warning.

"Great. So what are we waiting for?"

He was trying really hard not to smile, but she saw the telltale twitch at the corner of his mouth. "You need to think about it." He made his voice deadly serious. "You need to consider all the crap you've been through and whether it's a good idea to get something going on the rebound like this."

Feeling perfectly serene, she gave herself a slow count of five before answering, "Okay. I've thought about it. It's a good idea. A *really* good idea."

He took her by the shoulders and set her away from him. "Think about it some more."

She didn't argue. There was no need. The man was hers. He just couldn't let himself admit it.

Yet.

Chapter Six

Half an hour after Garrett left the house that morning, Cami got a call from her mother. The call didn't surprise her. Charles would have reported to her dad and her dad would have turned right around and sicced her mom on her.

Cami's mom was actually a nice woman. If not for Cami's dad, Hazel Lockwood would long ago have backed off and let Cami lead her own life.

The conversation went pretty much as expected. Her mom gently pleaded for her to be "reasonable" and return home immediately. Cami calmly explained that her home was now Justice Creek and she fully intended to make a new life there. She repeated what she'd told Charles, that she was not coming to Denver for a while and she did not want any visits from her parents. She asked that her parents respect her wishes and let her be for now and hung up feeling sad that it had come to this, but reasonably confident that they would leave her alone—for a while at least.

For the rest of the morning, she sat out on the deck, filling blank pages with sketches and ideas. She needed to focus on her next step in the process of creating a new and more satisfying way of life and she did her best thinking with a sketchbook in her hand.

When she got hungry, she made a sandwich from stuff left over from the cabin. Garrett's cupboards were looking kind of bare, so she texted him that she would get groceries and he should let her know anything specific he wanted. He texted back the usual guy-type items: beer, boxed cereal, chips, cheese and hamburger.

She replied, I'm cooking myself dinner. Should I make enough for you?

Absolutely. I'll be back by seven.

She was grinning to herself at the hominess of it all, the two of them texting each other about groceries and dinnertime, when her phone rang in her hand. It was the sheriff calling to let her know that she could go ahead and have her car towed out of the ravine.

Ten minutes later, feeling strong and capable and ready for anything her new life might hand her, she jumped in the Subaru and headed out to take care of business.

"Deck, I really don't know what to tell you, man." Garrett took a small sip of thirty-year-old scotch. It went down smooth with just enough heat. Normally, he didn't drink at lunch, not with a whole afternoon of work ahead of him. But Declan McGrath had ordered scotch. To be sociable, Garrett had said he'd have one, too.

They sat in a quiet back booth on the ground floor of McKellan's Pub, which was owned and managed by a family friend, Ryan McKellan—really, Rye was more like an actual member of the Bravo family. His brother Walker had married a Bravo cousin, Rory. Rye and Garrett's half sister Clara were lifelong best friends and had almost gotten married once. And four years ago, Rye had hired Bravo Construction to build a couple of loft apartments in the empty third floor above the pub. Rye lived in the front loft now with his new girlfriend, Meg. Nell had the one in the back.

"I can't catch a break with her." Deck meant Nell. Shaking his head, he turned his drink in a slow circle. "Why won't she act as the general on my new house? It's just business, right? What's wrong with my money, that's what I want to know?"

Garrett tried kidding him. "Dude. Nell doesn't want to run the project for you, but we'll still take your money."

Deck only grumbled, "Is that supposed to be funny?"

Might as well give it to him straight. "Nell says no, Deck. If we build your house, she's not running the project. And when Nell says no, you'd best take her word for it."

Deck raised his glass and knocked back a mouthful. "Well, I'm not giving up. One way or another, I'm going to get her to see that I know how wrong

I was and I'll do just about anything for one more chance with her."

Garrett sipped scotch and wondered idly what the deal was with Deck, to decide he had to try again with the high school sweetheart he'd dumped all those years and years ago? But Garrett didn't ask. He liked Deck and wanted his business, but no way was he ending up running interference between his sister and her old flame.

Nope. Not getting involved in their drama. Deck was one determined guy. But when Nell made up her mind about something, no mere man was likely to change it. They would have to fight this out on their own.

The waitress came with club sandwiches. They spent a few minutes concentrating on the food. Garrett's mind wandered a little—to Cami and that bone-melting kiss she'd given him earlier. He probably shouldn't have kissed her. It only made him want to kiss her some more and that wouldn't be wise. She needed a friend now, not more romantic complications.

And he needed to keep his grabby hands off.

He smiled to himself. She'd texted that she was cooking him dinner. The thought of that, of her in his kitchen whipping up a meal, made him smile. He did love having her around.

Did he love it too much?

No, he decided. He just needed to watch himself around her, keep it friends-only, and everything would be fine.

Deck said glumly, "So I'll bring the architect's plans by your office tomorrow morning? You can work up a contract for me."

Garrett swallowed a bite of sandwich. "You sure about this?"

"What? Nell or my new house?"

Garrett grunted. "Either. Both."

"Yeah. I'm sure. As for Nell and me, I'm not giving up. And even if she won't work with me personally on it, I still want Bravo Construction to build my house."

By six-thirty that night, Cami had chicken in mushrooms and wine bubbling on the stove.

Garrett got home right on time. It was a warm evening, not a cloud in sight. They ate outside on the deck. He praised her chicken and she slipped more than one bite to Munch, who sat by her chair, soulful eyes begging her. Garrett talked about all the work he had to catch up on at Bravo Construction.

She tried not to be jealous that he had work he seemed to love. "Lucky you. I'm still doodling all day, trying to decide what to do next."

"You'll figure it out." He said it with confidence, so certain she would not only come up with a job that made her happy, but when she did, she would be amazing at it.

He made her feel capable and special. Her life just somehow made complete sense when Garrett was around.

Was she falling and falling hard for the guy? Oh, yes, she was.

And who was she kidding, really, with the whole "falling" routine?

She'd already fallen. She loved him—was *in* love with him.

So what if she'd just met him five days before?

Love was love, no matter how fast it happened. Sophisticated people, people who thought they knew better about how the world worked, how relationships worked—people like her father and Charles—they thought love at first sight was some silly romantic notion, that you had to know someone forever to even begin to call it love.

And okay, maybe there was some truth to the way others viewed love. She was willing to give them that. *Some* truth, but not all.

Because life and love were bigger than any one person's perception of them. And some people did fall in love at first sight. They fell and they kept falling, deeper and deeper, as they continued to discover the rightness of that love.

Some people were perfect candidates for love at first sight. And Cami knew now that she was one of those people, someone who was finally getting her chance to follow her heart, instead of trying to be what others thought she should be.

Looking back on that first night at the cabin, the truth came crystal clear to her now. She'd seen the light of his campfire through the darkness and followed it. From the first moment she saw him, when he bolted straight up out of his camp chair and dropped his hot dog in shock at the sight of her, she'd *known* this was the man for her.

Was she going to tell him that?

Not for a while. Not until he was ready to hear it. Garrett was an amazing guy but kind of a slow learner when it came to love and romance. She wouldn't push him. She would give him all the time he needed to realize he loved her, too.

As they finished up their meal, she considered bringing up the subject of kissing and when they would be doing more of that. But she was kind of hoping he might bring it up first—or maybe kiss her again, which would be way better than just talking about it.

He did neither.

They cleared the table, and he loaded the dishwasher. Then he said he had work to catch up on. He disappeared into his home office at the front of the house.

She got ready for bed. All comfy in yoga pants and a sleep shirt, she settled on the couch in the living room to watch TV and fill up more pages with doodles and drawings.

At half-past ten, he still hadn't come out of his office. It was just her and Munch streaming the second season of *Orphan Black*. She could almost start to suspect that he might be avoiding her. That only made her smile. He liked her too much to avoid her forever. And that kiss this morning? It had told her everything she needed to know. He not only liked her, he was into her. She would love to move on from the friend zone right now.

But if he needed time, she would just have to give it to him.

At some point, she must have dropped off to sleep.

When she woke up, Garrett was all around her, his powerful arms cradling her. They were moving, going up the stairs. She could hear the tapping of Munch's claws on the hardwood floor as he followed behind them.

She wrapped her arms around his neck and snuggled in against his broad chest. "Take me to your room. I want to sleep with you."

"Cami," he said. Just her name and nothing more, in that chiding tone that told her everything—that he wanted to take her to his bed with him.

But he was telling himself he shouldn't.

He stopped at the door to her room. She could feel his hesitation. He felt he should take her in there and put her in the bed he'd assigned to her.

But he didn't want to do that, not really. He only *thought* that he should, because of what had happened that morning.

Because of the kiss.

Because they were just friends and he thought they ought to remain that way.

Wrong.

"Please." She breathed the word into the warm crook of his neck. "I promise not to try to kiss you."

A low sound escaped him. She felt the rumble of it in his chest. He was trying not to laugh.

And she snuggled in closer. Yeah, okay, she was shameless. She was also enjoying herself immensely. She had a new life to live and a fabulous man to seduce.

In time. When he was ready.

For now, though, she only wanted to sleep with him every night, to be close to him in the dark, where it would be easier to continue the bedtime talks they'd shared at the cabin. Easier to reveal the secrets of their hearts.

He stood there at her door for a minute or two that seemed to stretch out into eternity. She pressed her lips together to keep from coaxing him some more.

If he really didn't want her in his bed for whatever reason, she needed to accept that. Somehow.

But then at last, he continued on down the hall to the master suite. Happiness surged through her as he carried her in there and around the bed to the side she'd slept on the night before.

So gently, he laid her down and tucked the extra blanket around her. Munch jumped up and took his place down by the footboard.

Garrett disappeared into the bathroom. She heard the toilet flush and water running in the sink. Her eyes felt deliciously heavy. She shut them again and let sleep carry her away.

When Garrett came out of the bathroom, she was sound asleep, turned on her side, hands tucked under her cheek, a little smile on those plump lips of hers, his own scrappy little angel.

His own.

She wasn't, not really. He kept trying to remember that. But she was so adorable. Irresistible, really.

Whatever she wanted, all she had to do was ask. And he would scramble to get it for her.

He kept trying to remember all the reasons he shouldn't let her get too close. But somehow, with Cami, all the reasons added up to nothing. With Cami, half the time he couldn't even remember what those reasons were.

Ordinarily, he was a distant guy, a careful guy. A guy who mostly tried to keep interactions on a casual level. He got along with people just fine by not getting in too deep.

When it came to women, he liked a good time—in

and out of bed. A good time and not a lot more. After his marriage ended, he'd learned to keep things light. He'd accepted the fact that he didn't have what it took to make a real relationship work, that he was somehow emotionally disappointing, lacking in whatever it was a woman needed most from a man.

But then along came Cami.

With her, everything was all turned around. He felt scary-close to her. He loved just hanging with her. He *wanted* her living in his house.

Just look at him, *sleeping* with her without ever having had sex with her. What was that even about?

Her bruised eye opened halfway and she yawned. "You know it's weird that you're just standing there staring at me, right?" When he didn't answer immediately, she took one hand out from under her head and beckoned him down. "It's late. Come to bed."

Something happened inside him, a rising, warm sort of feeling. He didn't trust where this was going.

But so what? He was having a great time with her and helping her out a little, too. If she wanted to sleep with him, he wouldn't say no. She felt right in his bed, whatever they did or didn't do there.

And as far as keeping a little distance, keeping from getting *too* close, well, that would happen naturally. He worked long hours, after all. They would have plenty of time apart. And she would be busy making a whole new life for herself. It wouldn't be like on the mountain, just the two of them and Munch, together around-the-clock. The intensity of what they'd shared at the cabin would fade as time went by.

"Come to bed…" She said it even more softly that

time, on a sigh. Her hand was back under her cheek and her black eye had drifted closed.

Feeling eager to be closer to her and much too happy to have her sleeping in his bed, he switched off the lamp and slid in beside her.

Garrett left for work at seven the next morning. Cami barely had time to pour herself a first cup of coffee before he was out the door. About fifteen minutes later, the doorbell rang.

Cami peered through the window beside the door before opening it, just in case it might be Charles—or worse, her dad. Nope. A gorgeous redhead in jeans and heavy boots with bright tattoos on one arm saw her and waved. Something about the woman reminded Cami of Garrett. One of his sisters, maybe. Or possibly that cousin he'd mentioned once.

Cami pulled the door wide. "I'm sorry. Garrett's already left for work."

"Perfect. I wanted to get you alone. It's Cami, right? I'm Garrett's sister, Nell."

Cami felt a smile bloom. "You're the one nobody messes with."

"That's me."

"It's so good to meet you." She ushered Nell inside.

They had coffee on the sofa in the living room, while Munch snoozed on the rug in a wedge of early-morning sun.

Nell asked how she got the black eye and Cami ended up telling Garrett's sister everything—or, at least, most of everything, including the real story of how she and Garrett had met, from fleeing her wedding to the accident on the steep road, to wandering up Moosejaw Mountain barefoot in her wedding gown until she stumbled on Garrett and Munch at the cabin. "I'm starting my life over, I guess you could say. Garrett's helping me with that. He's invited me to stay here for as long as I need a place."

"He's nuts about you," Nell said.

Cami's heart did the happy dance. "He told you that?"

"No." Cami's face must have fallen. Nell explained, "He didn't have to tell me. I've known him all my life. He wouldn't invite just any woman to live with him. And when he talks about you, he gets that look." She made a silly face. "The man is gone on you."

Cami might be in love with the guy, but he wasn't there yet and she needed to respect that, so she downplayed what she felt for him. "We're good friends."

"Oh, I'll just bet you are." Nell chuckled.

Cami couldn't resist adding, "Your mother thinks we're a thing."

"Why am I not surprised?"

"Garrett tried to set her straight, but I didn't let him. I told her we were together—I mean, *really* together. I seriously got into it, too. Until he gave up and let me lie to her. I suppose I should feel guilty about that."

"Are you kidding? Why?" Nell laughed. "And whatever it is between you and Garrett, I'm glad. Ma drives us all batcrap crazy half the time, but she's right about Garrett. He's gotten to be way too much of a loner the last few years. He's a charmer and a good guy and most people don't even realize he never really gets close."

"But he does get close, Nell. *I* feel close to him."

"And you have no idea how glad I am to hear that."

Before she left, Nell invited Cami out for happy hour that evening at McKellan's Pub. Cami wanted to start meeting people in her new hometown, so she said yes.

"I'll make some calls," Nell said, "see how many of my brothers and sisters I can scare up. It'll be Bravos for days." Nell got out her phone and they exchanged numbers.

"I'll call Garrett," Cami said, "and invite him, too."

"Go for it."

As soon as Nell was out the door, Cami sent him a text and then waited with the phone in her hand, half expecting him to text her right back. He didn't. And she refused to feel let down as she slipped the phone into her purse. She put on enough makeup to cover her black eye and took Munch for a nice walk.

When she got back, she checked her phone. He'd answered, Sorry. On the run all day and then an early dinner with a wholesale carpet rep. Doubt I'll make McKellan's. Have fun.

So then. They wouldn't be having dinner together, either. He hadn't been kidding when he said he worked a lot. She tamped down her disappointment and texted back, All right. I'll just go have fun without you, then. See you later tonight.

She also had a voice mail from her dad. It was the usual, brief and unpleasant.

"Camilla, your behavior is completely unacceptable. I want you to come home and work things out with Charles. We don't need to discuss this. You just need to remember your responsibilities and start to live up to them. Call me immediately to tell me you're coming home."

The voice mail just made her want to ignore him and get on with her day. Too bad there was still a good girl lurking down inside her ready to ask, "How high?" when Quentin Lockwood said, "Jump." That girl would be edgy all day if she didn't reply.

However, talking to her dad never seemed to go well.

She settled on a text: Got your message. I live here in Justice Creek now and Charles and I are not getting back together. I will let you know when I plan to come to Denver. I'm not going to reply to any more of your demands, Dad. I love you and I'll be in touch.

Her heart beat a harsh rhythm under her ribs and her hands were shaking a little as she hit Send. She did love her dad and she knew he loved her, too. But the life he wanted for her, the life he'd so insistently seen she was groomed for, just wasn't a life that worked for her.

Really, she hated defying him. But if defiance was the price of her freedom, she would defy the hell out of her father until he finally saw the light.

She grabbed her keys and headed out the door.

Garrett worked in the office all morning. He met with Deck McGrath, discussed his house plans and promised him a bid within the next few days. Nell came in later from a renovation she was running up in Haltersham Heights.

"I stopped by your house and met Cami this morning," she said. "I like that girl." A buzz of annoyance sizzled through him. What made Nell think it was a good idea to go dropping in on Cami out of the blue?

Nell asked, "She get with you about coming to happy hour tonight at McKellan's?"

"Yeah." He stared blankly at his laptop screen and kept his voice noncommittal. "I don't think I'll make it."

Nell plunked her butt on the edge of his desk. "Why not?"

"I've got dinner at five with the new guy from Clarkson's Carpeting."

She leaned closer and peered over the top of the screen at him. "Reschedule with the carpet guy—or bring him along. C'mon. It'll be fun. And Cami's your girl. You really ought to be there."

His girl? No, she was not.

True, he couldn't seem to stop thinking about her and he'd already let her convince Ma that there was more going on between them than there was.

But that didn't make her his girl in any real sense.

She *wasn't* his girl. And he was putting a little distance between them as a way of reminding them both that they were just friends.

Because he really did need to draw the line somewhere. Didn't he? "What do you mean, *my* girl?"

Nell just stared at him, eyes like green daggers, for a few never-ending seconds. "You know exactly what I mean."

"What did Cami say to you?"

And then Nell smiled—a smile so sweet a guy could get a cavity just looking at it. "She said you two are friends. The *best* of friends."

"What the—?"

"Chill. She made it clear that it's friends-only, if that's what you're working up steam about."

He should have felt relief, right? But no. Now he felt sad and deflated to learn she *hadn't* tried to tell his sister that she was his girl.

Something was wrong with him. Cami had been so right when she told Ma he was messed up.

"We are," he said flatly. "Friends. Just friends."

"Well, great, then. Jacob Selby said he'd be there." Jacob was one of their subcontractors, a custom cabinet maker they used whenever possible for high-end builds and renos. The guy was six-six with long hair and a beard—and a striking resemblance to Chris Hemsworth. "I'm going to introduce them. You never know. They might hit it off."

No effing way. "Why?"

"Garrett." Nell's eyes twinkled with challenge. "Jacob's a sweetheart, which means the real question is, why not?"

"She doesn't need more complications in her life right now."

"I get that. And Jacob wouldn't be a complication. He's a total gentleman in the old-school sense of the word."

Garrett shut his laptop so he could glare at his sister unobstructed. "You are really pissing me off."

"And you've got your head up your butt. You've got a thing for that girl and you might as well just admit it, go with it. Who knows what might happen? Maybe something good."

"You're starting to sound like Ma now. It's not cute. And while we're on the subject of people with their heads up their butt, why have you got me running interference with poor Deck?"

Nell jumped off the desk like it was on fire. Her

red hair fanned out as she whirled on him. "That's low. You know it is."

"Why not just go with it?" He threw her own words back at her. *"Who knows what might happen? Maybe something good."* Yeah, he was acting like a ten-year-old. And right now, he didn't even care.

"Really? Seriously?" Nell demanded. "You're going *there*?"

"You bet I am."

"And you'd better stop. Deck already ripped my heart out of my body and ate it for lunch. Twice. I don't need that. Never again."

"That was in high school. Deck had it rough in high school."

"Didn't we all?"

"Don't. Yeah, we had our big family drama. But it was nothing like Deck's situation. The poor guy didn't know where his next meal was coming from—and whatever happened with you two back then, you're both different people now."

"Not that different. Let it go, Garrett."

"Then get off my back about Cami."

Nell pressed her lips together and seethed. But only for a moment. Finally, she gave it up. "Sure. Have it your way."

And don't you even try to set her up with Jacob. The words burned his tongue trying to get out, but somehow he held them back.

Nell left.

He had his assistant, Shelly, bring in takeout for lunch and ate at his desk as he continued to plow through the mountain of work that had piled up in his absence. In the afternoon, he made the rounds of current Bravo Construction projects. He met with his sister-in-law Chloe, an interior designer who was staging the model condo on a just-completed twelve-unit project on Aspen Way and had to read the riot act to a drywall subcontractor who was two weeks behind schedule on two BC jobs.

The whole time he was feeling like a complete jerk because he'd lied to Cami and to his sister. There was no early dinner with the carpet guy and he could definitely make it to McKellan's for drinks.

Hell. He *wanted* to meet Cami for Friday night happy hour.

He'd just had this feeling he ought to put the brakes on a little. But lying was a lousy way to do that.

If he really wanted to get some distance from her, he ought to try not carrying her to his bed at night. Or hey. What about just saying he was sorry, it wasn't working out for her to stay with him, after all? She'd made it clear that she could afford a place of her own. She didn't *need* to stay with him.

But again, he wanted her in his bed, whatever the two of them did or didn't do there. And he didn't want her to move out.

He wanted *her*. A lot. So much it scared him, so much he was mucking everything up. So much he was lying to her, fighting with Nellie about her, obsessing all day over her.

One way or another, this crap had to stop.

Dressed in tight white jeans, a flowy boho top and green suede cutout lace-up stilettos, Cami felt more like her new, freer, happier self than ever as she entered McKellan's Pub at five that night. So what if

Garrett wouldn't be there? She looked like a million bucks and she was going to meet some Bravos and have a great time.

Nell found her at the door, got her a drink and introduced her around. She met two of the Bravo brothers and Nell and Garrett's half sister Clara. Clara owned a restaurant over by the library. Her husband, Dalton Ames, was the president of Ames Bank.

Dalton, who was tall and dark-haired with killer blue eyes, knew Cami's parents. He said that before he moved to Justice Creek, he used to run into them now and then at charity events in Denver.

"Are you involved with WellWay, then?" he asked.

"Not anymore," she replied. "And never again."

Cami met the owner of the bar, Ryan. Rye was blond and hunky, one of those guys who could really turn on the charm. He joked that he and Nell were not only family in every way that mattered, they were next-door neighbors, living in adjoining loft apartments on the top floor of the building.

"Meg!" Nell signaled one of the bartenders, a tall, curvy woman with light brown hair. Meg stepped up on the other side of the bar and Nell introduced her to Cami.

Rye announced proudly, "Meg is with me." He caught Meg's hand where a diamond engagement ring glittered. "We're making it legal. I'm the happiest man in Colorado. She just said yes."

Meg held the ring up for Cami to see.

"It's beautiful. Congratulations."

Rye and Meg shared a glance full of love and desire and simple, open affection.

"Let's get a table," Nell suggested. She led Cami

to a deuce at the base of the stairs leading up to the second-floor bar.

Once they were seated, Nell explained that, until Meg, Rye had never gotten serious about a woman. "Except for Clara, back in the day. But Clara's happily married now and Rye's been, well, the way Rye's always been, which is one pretty girl after another. Until about a month ago, when Meg Cartwell's '56 DeSoto broke down a few miles east of town. Rye was driving back from Denver and stopped to help her out. Meg had left Denver herself, as it turned out. She was on her way home to Oregon, to this little seaside town right near the Washington border called Valentine Bay where—wait for it—her BFF since childhood is named Aislinn. Aislinn Bravo."

Cami laughed in delight. "A relative?"

Nell nodded. "A cousin. Aislinn's dad and my dad were brothers—so anyway, Rye talks Meg into sticking around for a while. With him." She pointed at the ceiling. "Upstairs. Meg had worked as a bartender, so he offered her a job. The man's totally in love and so is Meg. I never thought I'd see the day. It's happening fast. He proposed last night. I didn't even know she'd said yes until about an hour ago."

"Wow. That is pretty fast."

"I know. But fast just works for some people."

"Oh, Nell. I so agree. My life has been way too controlled, everything laid out, planned ahead. Never making a move without considering every angle. Every decision reached with long deliberation. I like life a little more on the fly, you know? Especially when it comes to love. I mean, you may not really be able to love a person at first sight. But you can know if you *could* love them. You can see the potential. And I would take it even further. I would say that when it comes to love, sometimes your heart just *knows*."

"Yes!" Nell raised her hand, palm out, above the table. Cami slapped hers against it in a high five. Then Nell said, "I never thought Rye would ever find the one for him. It wasn't like he was looking for someone, if you know what I mean. But then he met Meg. That was it. She's the one. They both seem really sure. I think it's going to work out for them."

Cami was nodding. "Seeing them together, I have to agree."

"They're getting married at Christmastime. I can't wait. I already love Meg like one of my sisters. And you gotta know that cousin Aislinn will be coming out from Oregon to be Meg's maid of honor. We might have a mini Bravo family reunion along with a holiday wedding."

"It's so romantic." Cami thought a little wistfully of Garrett, who couldn't be here tonight because he had a date with a carpet salesman. She shouldn't be so disappointed not to have him here—and she *wasn't*. She refused to be. She focused on enjoying the moment, on being with Nell, girlfriends together, having a good time on Friday night.

Nell waved at a big, long-haired, bearded guy in jeans, lumberjack boots and a flannel shirt. "Jacob! Over here." She grabbed a chair from the next table.

The big guy came and loomed above them. "Nell." He saluted her with a tall glass of dark beer. "How's it going?"

Nell patted the chair and Jacob sat down. She introduced him to Cami. Jacob had warm hazel eyes and a friendly smile. He was a carpenter, he said, and did work for Bravo Construction.

Nell spotted one of her brothers over by the bar. "There's Carter. I'll be right back."

And off she went, leaving Cami with Jacob, who was really nice and seemed to be flirting with her. He asked her how she liked Justice Creek.

She told him just how she felt about the place. "I love it here, Jacob. I've decided I'm not leaving. I'm making Justice Creek my home."

"A woman who knows what she wants." He leaned a little closer. "I like that." He asked her more questions.

She didn't get into too much detail, but she told him the basics, that she was staying in Justice Creek and looking around for business opportunities. He talked about his work. His dad, he said, had been a carpenter before him.

Jacob was easy to talk to. She was starting to think that maybe she'd made a new friend.

And then she glanced up and spotted Garrett. Her skin got all shivery and her heart gave a happy little lurch beneath her breastbone. "Garrett!" She stuck up her hand and waved him over.

Not that she needed to. He was already on his way, staring straight at her, the corners of his sexy mouth turned down in a grim, angry line.

Chapter Seven

Jacob turned in his chair to see Garrett coming toward them—and Garrett's hostile expression morphed instantly into something borderline friendly. Jacob got up. "Garrett. Hey."

"Jacob." The men shook. When Jacob sat back down, Garrett took the chair Nell had left vacant.

Cami regarded him across the table. She was so glad to see him here—and yet suspicious, too. Something strange was up with him, scowling one minute, then putting on a smile. She just didn't get it. "No dinner with the carpet guy, after all?"

Garrett answered offhandedly. "Yeah, didn't happen."

Jacob frowned and glanced back and forth between her and the infuriating man across the table. "Carpet guy?"

"Cami wanted me here tonight." Garrett's gaze stayed locked with hers. "But I had a business dinner."

Wanted? Well, yeah. She had. She *did*. But the way he said it made it sound like she'd begged him to come.

She glared right back at him. "I *invited* you."

"Because you *wanted* me."

This was getting really weird. Cami felt angry and kind of turned on, both at once. She really had no idea what to say next.

And poor Jacob. He looked like he just wanted out of there. Fast. Cami so didn't blame him.

"Okay, guys." Jacob put up both hands. "Is there something I'm missing here?"

Cami tried a laugh. It came out sounding strained. "Garrett and I are good fr—"

"Cami and I live together."

Talk about a conversation stopper. Cami actively resisted the burning need to give him a good, sharp kick under the table. Could he be any ruder? Let alone more confusing?

Above his beard, Jacob's cheeks had flushed dark red. Apparently, he really had been flirting with her. And now Garrett had made him feel like a fool. "Look, guys. I'm not here to make any trouble. Nell didn't tell me you two were a couple."

Garrett gave a lazy shrug. "You know Nell. She loves to stir things up."

Cami should have jumped in right there and insisted that Nell hadn't stirred anything up and she and Garrett *weren't* a couple. But then again, being with Garrett was just what she wanted, so denying that they were a couple would be counterproductive to her own heart's desire.

In the end, she said nothing. She just sat there with her mouth shut, feeling all turned around, half of her gleeful that Garrett seemed to be claiming her. And half of her pissed off that he had to be such a complete douchenozzle about it.

Jacob had had enough. "Looks to me like the two of you need to talk." He stood.

Cami gazed up at him. He seemed like such a good guy, with his kind eyes and that gentle, friendly way he had. She liked him—but he wasn't Garrett. And she and Garrett really did need to talk. "Great to meet you, Jacob."

The big man gave a nod and left them alone. The minute he was gone, Garrett shifted to stand. "Want another drink?"

"Don't you dare run off now." She pinned him with her hardest glare until he sank back into the chair.

"I was just getting a drink." He said it so mildly. Apparently, mean, surly Garrett had vanished. In his place sat easygoing, evenhanded Garrett, aka the amazing man she'd met on the mountain.

"Drinks can wait." She sat back in the chair and crossed her arms over her chest. "You realize you just made me look like a cheater."

"A cheater?" He put on a look of great surprise.

"Yes. A cheater. That is what I said."

"Cami, what are you talking about?"

"Oh, please. You're trying to tell me you honestly don't get it?"

"Get what?"

"You are really pushing it, you know that? But

just in case you actually do need help with this, allow me to explain. Before you got here, Jacob was flirting with me."

"Yeah." Now he sounded surly again. "I picked up on that. Loud and clear."

"Jacob was flirting with me and I was letting him—because *you* have made it painfully clear to me that you and I are *not* together. Feel free to correct me if I've got that wrong."

"Cami, hey…" He leaned in and folded his beautiful, strong hands on the table. Faint white scars marked his knuckles, testament to the hard work he'd done with those hands. She wanted to touch them, to touch *him*. All over. Too bad at the moment she also wanted to jump up and walk out. He gave her the melty eyes. "Don't be pissed at me."

"But I *am* pissed at you." She leaned across the table, too, folding her hands on it, same as him. "You had better start being honest with me, Garrett Bravo, or I am getting up from this chair and walking out of here."

He looked down at the table, then over at the bar, then across at the retro neon beer sign on the opposite wall. Anywhere but at her. She waited, giving him one more chance to start making things right.

And then, at last, he confessed, "I felt like we were getting too close."

She clasped her hands tighter—to keep them from reaching out to him. "Got that. Keep going."

"When you texted me about tonight, I wanted to meet you here. I wanted it bad. To be out with you, us together, and not just as friends."

Joy burned through her, silvery and fine. "I wanted that, too."

"But I was afraid. So I lied and made up the dinner meeting with the carpet guy."

Her joy kind of fizzled as disappointment dragged on her, that he'd fabricated a business dinner in order to put distance between them. "I appreciate that you're admitting you lied to me. But Garrett, if you want a little space or whatever, you need to just say so."

"But that's just it. I *didn't* want space. I wanted to get closer and that freaked me out. And you're right about the lying. It's not a solution to anything. I never should have lied to you. I am sorry, Cami." He held her eyes as he said it.

And that did it. She forgave him.

Why hold out against him? She'd wanted him to come with her tonight, and now, here he was, admitting at last that there was more than just friendship between them. She wasn't exactly thrilled with how they'd gotten here.

But at least they *were* here.

She gave him a slow nod. "I accept your apology." Her fingers just wouldn't stay still. They inched across the smooth wood of the tabletop until they touched his. She waited, breath held. And then his big hand closed around hers, warm and rough and so very right. Her heart was just galloping away inside her chest. She asked, "What are you afraid of?"

He didn't answer right away. She started to think he would blow off the question. But then he said, "Right now, you don't need a new boyfriend. You need someone you can count on. We're supposed to be friends and I'm supposed to be helping you. Instead,

I'm thinking all the time about getting you naked—and *you're* not helping *me* to remember what a bad idea that would be."

"But Garrett. It wouldn't be bad. I happen to think it could be very, very good."

He glared at her. "See? Like I said, you're not helping."

"Garrett, I want to be with you, *really* be with you. And since you want that, too, we don't even have a problem except for the one you've made up in your head."

"What if it all goes to hell?" He regarded her warily now. At least he'd stopped glaring. "I don't have the best record when it comes to the whole romance thing. I'm no good at relationships."

"Who told you that? Wait. Let me guess. Your ex-wife?"

"Yeah, and my ex and I didn't agree on a lot of things, but about this, she was right."

"Sorry, not buying that. And come on, lighten up. We like each other. A lot. I want us to take the next step together, that's all. It's not like I'm asking for a lifetime commitment." *Not yet, anyway.*

"You're impulsive."

"I know." She allowed herself a slow grin. "I love that about me. Taking things slowly? Thinking everything over in advance? If that floats your boat, more power to you. But to me it's just an excuse not to reach out and grab hold of what you really want."

He was still looking grim. "At least one of us should be considering the consequences."

"But I *am* considering the consequences. And the way I see it, whatever happens in the future, we have something good, you and me. We have something good and I want to go with it, to see where it takes us."

"You know who you sound like?" He was still way too serious. "Nell. She came in the office this morning and got on me about you, about how it was obvious I wanted you and you wanted me. She said that I should go for it with you."

Cami crowed out a happy laugh. "Okay, just for the record, I love Nell." He actually smiled. At last. And then she demanded, "What else did Nell say?"

"She threw Jacob into the mix, told me how she was going to introduce you two tonight. I said she'd better not try it. And she started in about how Jacob's such a prince and if I don't want you for myself, what do I care if she introduces the two of you?" He lifted her hand off the table and put his other hand around it, too, surrounding her in the thrilling heat of his touch. "I was miserable all day."

"Serves you right," she said tenderly.

"And then, well, here I am now because if I was a woman I would go out with Jacob. I couldn't stand the thought of him making a move on you." He asked glumly, "You would have said yes, right?"

"No."

He brightened. But then he scoffed, "Oh, come on. He's a great guy and he looks like Thor. Anyone would go for him—I mean, anyone who's into guys."

She wanted to kiss him, but for the moment she kept her lips to herself. "I like him. But that's all. I wouldn't have gone out with him. Can we please stop talking about Jacob now?"

"Works for me—and the thing is, I *wanted* to be here with you. Even if Nell hadn't threatened to dangle some serious man candy in front of you, I don't think I would have been able to stay away."

"I'm so glad." She leaned as far as she could across the table.

He looked at her as though he would never look away. "Cami..." And then he leaned in, too, just enough for a kiss, a sweet kiss, a swift, perfect brush of his lips across hers.

She sank back to her chair with a happy sigh.

They stayed on at McKellan's long past happy hour.

Garrett kept her close and Cami loved every minute at his side. She met more Bravo brothers and sisters, wives and husbands, and family friends, too.

Garrett's mother showed up. Everyone seemed blown away that Willow had a guy with her, a lean, good-looking older man with thick white hair. She introduced the guy around. His name was Griffin Masters and he lived in San Diego.

She'd met him on one of her cruises, she said. "Griffin's staying for a few weeks."

Garrett looked a little stunned. "What? You mean, with you, at the mansion?"

Willow seemed to be restraining herself from rolling her eyes. "Yes, Garrett. With me."

As soon as Willow led her new boyfriend away, Garrett said, "I don't believe this. Ma with a guy. I don't think she's been with anyone since Dad died. I never thought she would."

Cami didn't get it. "Would what?"

"I don't know. Be with anyone who wasn't Dad."

"Didn't you say it's been six years since your father died?"

"Yeah. So?"

"So then, she's moving on, slowly getting over the loss of her husband. That's a good thing, don't you think?"

He looked kind of stunned. "You don't get it. She started with my father when she was eighteen. There was never anyone else for her." Over at the bar, Willow lifted her martini and touched it to Griffin's glass. The glance they shared sizzled with heat.

Cami gently suggested, "Well, it looks like there's definitely someone else now."

Garrett grabbed her hand. "There's a bar upstairs. Let's go up there."

She hung back. "Um. Because?"

"She's my mother. She's always made me crazy, what with her stealing another woman's husband, all the yelling and carrying on when we were kids and then marrying my dad when Sondra was barely dead. Not to mention taking Sondra's mansion and everything in it and making it her own. And then lately with all the matchmaking. And now *this*." He tipped his head toward his mother and her boyfriend, who were sharing a kiss. "Look at that. I didn't need to see that." He pulled Cami toward the stairs.

She followed, arguing, "Garrett, she's a vibrant, beautiful woman. You should be happy for her."

He only muttered, "I think my eyeballs are scarred for life," and led her up the steps.

At the upstairs bar, there was more excitement.

Nell was giving some serious grief to a big, hot-looking guy in a suit. "You don't fool me, Declan McGrath. I know what you're up to and it's not going to work."

The big guy answered mildly, "Sparky, get over yourself. I'm just having a drink."

Cami pulled Garrett closer. "Sparky?"

He put his wonderful warm lips to her ear and explained, "Pet name from the old days. They used to be together years ago. He wants another chance with her. Nell says no, but Deck won't give up."

Nell had more than no to say. "You don't need to get your drinks here." He sat with his back to her, facing the bar. She leaned over his shoulder. "Go to some other bar."

"Relax." He slowly sipped what looked like whiskey, neat.

"Damn you, Deck. I *live* here."

"This is a bar. I'm what is known as a customer. You live upstairs."

"You are harassing me and I am sick of it."

Elise Walsh, one of the Bravo sisters, came up on Garrett's other side. She suggested out of the corner of her mouth, "You take Deck and I'll take Nell."

"Crap," said Garrett wearily. "Sure."

"I'll go in first."

"Have at it."

Elise, looking cool and professional in a pencil skirt and silk top, glided to Nell's side. She took Nell's arm and whispered something in her ear. Nell scowled, but she did let Elise pull her away as Garrett grabbed a chair for Cami.

"Sit here," he said. "I'll be right back with drinks."

She took the chair and grinned up at him. "No hurry. I'll just enjoy the show."

But apparently, the show was over. Garrett slid onto the stool beside the man named Deck. He leaned close and said something. The big man muttered something back, threw some bills on the bar and left.

"Life with the Bravos is so exciting," Cami said when Garrett returned with fresh drinks. "I love this town. Did I mention I'm never going to leave?"

"I think you did, and more than once." He bent close and kissed her and she thought, *This is happiness*. Together with Garrett on a Friday night.

Around eight, they ordered burgers. Rye and Meg joined them. Then later, Nell invited the four of them upstairs to her loft, which was gorgeous and open, all modern and sleek.

It was after midnight when Garrett walked Cami to her Subaru in the parking lot in back.

At the car, he framed her face in his hands. "Tonight was good." His woodsy scent tempted her and his warm breath touched her cheek.

"More than good. Because we were together. Really together, for the first time."

He kissed her, a slow kiss, a kiss that got hotter and deeper the longer it went on. She heard footsteps behind her somewhere. A woman laughed low. A car door opened and then shut. All that was nothing compared to the pleasure of Garrett's mouth on hers. She felt the lovely, hard ridge of him, wanting her, pressing into her belly.

When he finally lifted his head, she let her eyes drift open and gave him a slow smile. "A good-night kiss…"

A low rumble of laughter escaped him. "Except it's not good-night because you're coming home with me."

"Where's your car?"

"Two rows over." He smoothed a hank of hair behind her ear.

"I'll wait for you."

He kissed her again, even deeper than the first time, his body so hard and hot, pressed against her. Most of her life, she'd felt she was missing out on the good stuff somehow.

Not anymore. She had her arms around Garrett now. And she was following him home.

At the house, they greeted Munch and took him out into the yard. He bustled around, sniffing the bushes, chasing after shadows. She and Garrett sat together on the end of the low deck. The moon was a full silver ball floating above the mountains, the stars a little faded-looking, paled by the lights of town.

Garrett put his arm around her and pulled her in close. She rested her head on his shoulder. It seemed to her the best place to be in the whole world—on the deck with Garrett, the moon so big and magical, shining in the sky.

He said, "It's a week tomorrow night since you appeared out of nowhere up on my mountain."

"Only a week? Not possible. It seems like forever that I've known you."

He ran his hand down the outside of her arm, a slow caress that set a thousand fluttery creatures loose in her belly. "I want to take you to bed with me. And not just as roomies."

"Yes."

He nuzzled her hair and teased, "You are so easy."

"Yes, I am and proud of it." She put her hand on his chest, felt his heartbeat, strong and steady beneath his shirt, under warm flesh and sturdy bone. "Tell me about your ex."

He chuckled low. "Now, there's a mood killer."

She poked him, just a little, with her elbow. "Come on. I want to know."

"I don't know what to tell you."

"How about her name, to start?"

"Miranda Hale. She's a teacher."

"Does she still live here in Justice Creek?"

"No. She moved to Milwaukee after our divorce. Her family's there. But when I met her, she was teaching third grade at Justice Creek Elementary. Nell and I were just getting Bravo Construction off the ground. Miranda hired us to remodel her kitchen."

"And you asked her out?"

He nodded. "We got married about a year later. She was pregnant." Cami blinked in surprise. It was the first time he'd mentioned having children. "I wanted the baby," he said. "And I wanted Miranda."

A baby. Cami had a thousand questions. Did Miranda take the child away from him? But how? That would be so awful. But the alternative was even worse.

She asked, "Were you happy—I mean, at first?"

"On and off. We always had issues, I guess you could say. I don't like drama, don't like it when things get messy and emotional. Miranda claimed that I was never 'emotionally available.' Her words. 'Garrett, you're just not emotionally available and I have no clue how to reach out to you.' She also used to say that there was no 'there' there with me."

Cami pressed a little closer to his side. "Your ex-wife was wrong."

"No. She was right. Ask anyone. My bet is they'll

say that they like me well enough. But they don't know me very well." He chuckled. The sound didn't have a lot of humor in it. "And I have no idea why you want to hear about Miranda and me. Believe me, I'm not the hero of that story."

"You're a hero to me. And I want to know the things you wouldn't tell just anybody."

He toyed with the filmy sleeve of her shirt and then carefully smoothed it down over her arm. "A few weeks after the wedding, Miranda said she knew I never would have married her if there hadn't been a baby. I lied and said that wasn't true. But she wasn't fooled." He fell silent.

Cami tipped her head up to look at him. He was staring at the moon.

Eventually, he spoke again. "At four months along, she lost the baby."

Oh, no. She pressed her hand to his heart again and sought his gaze through the darkness. "I'm so sorry, Garrett."

His eyes were full of shadows. But he brushed his lips to her temple in a tender little kiss. "I didn't know what to do about that, how to comfort her, you know?"

Cami allowed herself a small sound of understanding, but no more. He was talking to her, *really* talking. She would not miss a word.

He went on. "She tried to get me to go into counseling, but I said no. I worked even harder than usual, eighteen-hour days sometimes. She'd always said I didn't spend enough time with her. After we lost that baby, she said she hardly saw me at all. I would promise to be home more. And then there would always be some crisis that kept me working late.

"Then, three years after we lost the first baby, she got pregnant a second time. She cried when she told me. She said she shouldn't have gotten pregnant again, that it wasn't going to work with us, that just being with me made her lonely. And then, at five months along, we lost that baby, too."

Cami didn't know what to say. It was such a sad story. She ached for him. And for his ex-wife, too.

He gathered her closer against his side. "A year later, I came home from work one night and Miranda was gone. She left me a note. One line. *'Without the babies, what's the point?'* She sent me the divorce papers and I signed them. That's it. The story of my marriage that was probably doomed from the start."

Munch came and sat on his other side, settling in close, as though the dog knew his human needed support.

Cami said, "You blame yourself that it didn't work out." It wasn't a question.

And he didn't say she had it wrong. Instead, he fiddled with her hair, smoothing it, then wrapping a curl around his index finger. "I did marry her mostly because of the baby. I didn't love her enough. And she was always so emotional. Her tears didn't reach me—they only made me shut down, made me want to get away."

She gazed up at him, at his handsome face silvered in moonlight. She wanted so much to understand. "Because?"

"My childhood, I guess." He avoided meeting her eyes and stared off toward the dark humps of the mountains. Somewhere near the back fence, a night bird twittered. A slight breeze stirred the bushes and made the branches of the pine tree a few feet from the deck whisper together.

"You said tonight at McKellan's that your mother was emotional when you were growing up."

"Yeah. She likes to play it civilized and sophisticated now, with her martinis and the big, fancy house that used to be Sondra's. Now, she travels first-class and never raises her voice. But she wasn't always like that. When I was growing up, she was constantly carrying on, kicking my dad out of the house, then taking him back. I never wanted to live like that, with the endless shouting matches, the ongoing drama. And now..." He seemed to run out of words.

"Now, what?" she prompted.

"Now, looking back on the years with Miranda, I see that, yeah, she was emotional. But really, she was just trying to reach out to me and I kept pushing her away."

Cami stared up at the moon, too, thinking about all he'd just said. His honesty touched her. But he'd been too hard on himself, she thought. And she could guess why. "So you *are* saying it's your fault that your marriage failed, that you didn't love your wife enough and you were a terrible husband?"

"Yeah. That's about the size of it."

"Well, I don't agree with you."

He gave her a wry smile for that. "Cami. You get that it's really not up to you, right?"

"You lost *two* babies, Garrett. That's so awful. And not just for Miranda. For you, too. Sometimes a marriage just can't stand the weight of losses like that. And okay, I never met your wife, but I'll bet if I talked to her, she might have a few regrets about her part in what happened. I'll bet she wouldn't let you have *all* the blame."

He was actually smiling. "About that new career you're looking for? Maybe you ought to consider going into family counseling."

She didn't smile back. "Don't try to make light of what happened to you—and to Miranda. It seems to me that you grew and changed from it, that you see your part in what went wrong. I admire that. What I *don't* like is that this story, what you just told me, it's like a warning, isn't it? You're trying to scare me away."

"You *should* be scared." He was sounding all gruff and grumpy again.

She took his warm, beard-stubbled face between her two hands. "Stop trying to protect me from you. I don't *want* to be protected from you. I'm having the best time of my life with you and I don't want to stop. I *want* you. Now, tonight. And the only question right now is, do you want me, too?"

He looked at her for the longest time. And then, at last, he answered, "You know I do."

"Perfect." She threw her leg across him and climbed into his lap.

He groaned. "God. Cami…"

It was the sweetest, sexiest moment. She could feel him growing harder, right there at the core of her, and she had his unforgettable face tipped up to her.

Cami did what came naturally. She wrapped her arms around his neck and pressed her mouth to his.

Chapter Eight

Did she fear he would refuse her?

A little, yeah.

But he didn't. Instead, he gathered her closer. He wrapped his wonderful arms so tight around her and took the kiss deeper. She lost herself in it—in all of it. In his thrilling hardness and heat, in the wet, hot tangling of their seeking tongues and caressing hands.

And then his touch strayed down her back, dipping into the curve of her spine, sliding out over the flare of her hips, until he cradled her bottom. Holding her firmly, he shifted forward.

"Oh!" She wrapped her legs around him good and tight, hooking her stilettos at the small of his back as he rose.

And then they were kissing again, a dizzying kiss that went on and on as he strode across the deck to the glass door that led into the living room. When he got there, still kissing her, he reached out and shoved the door wide. Munch bumped through ahead of them. Garrett carried her in and she stuck out a hand to slide the door shut.

For a moment, he paused there just inside the door, holding her close to him, kissing her as though he couldn't get enough of the taste of her mouth. She kissed him right back, as hungry for him as he was for her.

And then he was moving again, across the living room into the front hall and on up the stairs.

He broke the kiss at the door to his bedroom. "Munch," he commanded. "*Your* bed. Lie down." With only one plaintive whine, Munchy trotted over to the dog bed in the corner and climbed in.

Garrett carried her into the room, over to the gorgeous barn-wood bed and on around to the side she already thought of as hers. Carefully, he lowered her until she stood on the rug. She swayed on her feet when he let her go.

He steadied her. "Okay?"

"Garrett, I am so far past okay. I'm splendid. I'm downright spectacular."

"Oh, yes, you are." His voice was a low rumble, his eyes low and lazy, just eating her up. She felt his gaze as a touch that burned and beckoned. "Do. Not. Move."

Staring into his beautiful eyes, she caught her lower lip between her teeth and nodded.

He turned, grabbed the covers and threw them back.

It sent a hot shiver all through her to see the white

sheets revealed. Tonight, there would be no blankets to separate them. Just the thought of the two of them naked together made her knees go all shaky in the most delicious way.

And seriously, before they went any further, she needed to tell him that she hadn't exactly done this before.

But then he commanded, in a voice so low and intimate, "Sit down. Right here." He bent and patted the sheet.

She couldn't drop to the bed fast enough. Never had she felt quite like this—breathless, her skin supersensitized, her face flushed with heat.

Garrett knelt at her feet. He wrapped his hand around the back of her calf. Even through her jeans, she felt his cradling touch so acutely, his fingers molding, caressing, as his hand glided down the back of her leg, stirring a chain of delicious shivers as it went.

He stopped at the spot where her heel met the back of her lace-up stiletto, cradling her foot as he undid the laces. "These are some dangerous shoes you got here, Camilla."

"Cami," she corrected a little more sharply than necessary, reaching out to brush her fingers through his hair. It was so thick and unruly, the richest brown color, warm and alive.

His head was tipped down, but she saw the corner of his mouth lift. "It pisses you off when someone calls you Camilla?"

"Yeah."

"Well, that gets me hot." He looked up and locked eyes with her again as he slid off that sandal. "But about these high-heeled shoes…"

"Hmm?"

He set the sandal neatly upright beneath the night table. "These shoes make a man want to see you wearing them with your legs in the air."

"Oh!" It came out on a goofy little gasp.

"Maybe I'll get to see that sometime."

"I… Sure," she answered dazedly. Because her mind was a hot stew, every neuron blazing. All he'd done was take off her shoe and suddenly she had no mental energy left to form coherent verbal responses.

But then again, it wasn't only the shoe. It was the searing looks he gave her, the way he'd carried her in here with her all wrapped around him, the endless, sizzling-hot kiss they'd shared.

He got busy with the other sandal, untying the laces, sliding it off. And finally setting it side by side with its mate under the nightstand. Then he rose to stand above her again. "Up, now."

She felt…hypnotized. Mesmerized. By his caramel eyes, by his rough-tender commands. She stood.

And then he was taking her filmy shirt and lifting it. "Raise your arms." She raised them. He pulled the shirt up and off. "So pretty…" He brushed a finger against the satin bow in the center of her lacy purple bra.

She just stared at him, eager and yearning and suddenly totally out of her depth. It was time—past time. She knew it. She *had* to open her mouth and tell him.

He cradled her breast.

It felt so good. She let out a tiny moan. "Um. I…"

He leaned closer. His warm breath touched her cheek as he whispered, "Beautiful," and slipped his thumb beneath the cup of her bra.

She made another sound. It wasn't a word, just a tiny squeak of pleasure as he brushed his thumb back and forth across her nipple.

And then he took her mouth. He kissed her slow and deep. His hands got busy. They roamed all over her, rubbing her shoulders, caressing her back, molding her waist and wrapping both hands around her bottom again, stroking, squeezing...

She returned his kiss eagerly. It felt so good, nothing better. He must have popped the hooks at the back of her bra. She lowered her arms and the bra fell away and vanished.

Poof.

She sighed as he cupped her bare breasts, one in each hand.

"Since that first night," he said low and rough in her ear as he touched her, caressing her, rubbing her nipples between his thumbs and forefingers. "You've been making me crazy. You, in that white corset thing, standing in the bathroom by the tub, and then on the porch after your bath in only a towel. Looking so good, so hot. Even with your eye bright purple, swollen shut, and most of you covered in scrapes and scratches, I wanted to eat you right up."

Did she moan out his name? It seemed that she might have.

"Kiss me, Cami."

Eagerly, she offered her mouth and he claimed it all over again, his hands on the move once more, straying down to the placket of her white jeans. The kiss took her over. She gave herself up to it—to him, with his skilled mouth and talented hands, his rough-tender words and the manly, clean scent of him that she would know in a room full of strangers, with all the lights off.

I should tell him, she scolded herself as he undid her fly and took her jeans down.

I need to tell him, she thought in a vague, distant way as he knelt and trailed a line of worshipful kisses along the white scar that ran the length of her thigh.

But she didn't tell him. He ruled her senses. And she really couldn't bear it if he stopped. And what would it be but a mood-killer, to tell him now that this was a first for her?

Uh-uh. She wanted this with all her heart and soul. She wanted *him*.

She did not want to stop now. And she knew him, she really did. Knew him to his soul already, in the space of a week. So what if that was impossible? It was also true.

If she told him, he would stop.

There would be talking. There would be slowing down and taking time and, well, she just didn't need time.

She needed him. She needed *this*. To be swept away, taken over, kissed and touched and claimed at last.

So she sighed and pulled him up to her and moaned in delight when he lifted her and laid her down, naked and yearning, on the white sheets of his bed.

He stripped and he was fast about it. In half a minute, he had everything off and tossed aside. Then he just stood there, unmoving, looking down at her through those golden eyes.

"Garrett…" He was so fine, with those broad, muscled shoulders, everything cut and hard and honed.

She drank him in, his square-jawed face and powerful neck, that tempting line of silky hair trailing downward from his broad chest, over his ridged belly all the way to where he was ready for her, thick and erect, big enough to scare her a little.

It would probably hurt.

But she didn't care. It wouldn't hurt for long. And she wanted him all over her, moving inside her, whispering her name.

All her life, she'd been looking. For *this* life, the life that he'd shown her, the life she'd waited too long to find. Everything was wide-open now. She could find her truest self, be the woman she was meant to be—Garrett's woman, she fervently hoped.

She reached up her arms to him.

With a slow smile, he took a condom from the bedside drawer and set it by the clock. "Cami." He said her name all rough and low, like a promise, like a secret they shared, just the two of them.

And he came down to her. She rolled to face him as he stretched out on his side. He touched her throat, smoothed her hair, whispered again that she was beautiful.

And she was perfectly, gloriously lost—in his touch, in the feel of his naked body against hers, in the rough scrape of his beard scruff, the taste of his mouth, the hot sweep of his tongue beyond her parted lips.

She could kiss him forever. Until their mouths fused permanently, never again to part.

He gave her bottom lip a little nip as he went lower, running that naughty tongue of his down the center of her throat. "You taste like heaven." He kissed the words onto the side of her neck.

And his kisses didn't stop there. On they went. He breathed one into the hollow her throat, scattered them across her upper chest until he reached the waiting curves of her breasts.

He lavished attention on one and then the other, taking her nipples into his mouth, sucking them deep.

She lay moaning in dizzy delight as he drove her wild with kisses, with slow, perfect caresses.

And no, she wasn't a complete innocent. She'd had boyfriends, fooled around. She really shouldn't let him do all the work here. She needed to take a little initiative, do more than just lie here in ecstasy, gasping and sighing, reveling in the glory of his every touch.

But she was lost in the best way, a slave to his stroking hands, to his skilled, hungry kisses.

Her breasts ached in the sweetest way as he kept kissing them, kept drawing her nipples into the wet heat of his mouth, making her clutch him close and cry out, "Yes!" and "Please," and "Don't ever stop."

He didn't stop.

He went farther. Lower.

His fingers strayed to the core of her, where she was wet and so ready for him. He stroked her, making low sounds of excitement and approval, those fingers of his strumming her, playing her just right.

He dipped a finger in. "You're so tight…"

She made a noise of agreement, self-reproach stirring. *I need to tell him…*

But she didn't. She eased her legs wider as he stroked her. She lifted her hips off the bed, inviting him, encouraging him, opening herself fully to the searing perfection of his touch.

He was just really good at this, taking his sweet time with her, caressing her so perfectly, kissing his way down her belly, so he could play her with his mouth and his wonderful fingers, together. It felt so good, exactly right.

She never, ever wanted it to end.

But he kept the pleasure building. And her climax took her over without warning.

She hit the peak, her body opening like a flower of purest sensation, pulsing as she came. The world was suddenly a bright, hot, expanding shimmer of light with her at the center, pleasure racing along every nerve ending, flying out the ends of her fingers, the tips of her toes—and then turning inward again, contracting down into the core of her, leaving her limp and satisfied, wearing a silly smile.

Garrett didn't think he'd ever seen anything as beautiful as Cami losing herself to his touch.

At the end, as she went loose and easy, he gathered her close to him and stroked her sunny, wildly tangled hair. She tucked her head into the crook of his neck and sighed in contentment.

"So good." Her soft lips brushed his throat.

And then her cool hand went roaming, her fingers trailing down the outside of his arm, along the line of his hip. A moment later, those soft fingers closed around him. He groaned, aching for more.

But he had questions that needed answering first. He caught her wrist. "Hey."

She made a questioning sound. But she did let go.

He brought her hand to his lips and kissed her sweet fingertips, lingering on the rough spot, that callus at the top inside joint of her middle finger where her pencil rested when she drew in those notebooks of hers. "You got something you want to talk to me about?"

Her sharp intake of breath said it all. And then she tipped her head back and stared at him through anxious eyes. A sweet blush crept up her slim neck and over her cheeks. "You can tell?"

"Not for sure. Not until a second ago, from that little sound you made when I asked, and the look on your face right now. And, well, you *are* really tight."

Her blush deepened. "I…didn't know how to say it. It felt so awkward just to blurt it out. And it was so beautiful, what you were doing. I thought maybe we could, you know, just go ahead and let it happen."

He hid a smile. "Get it over with, you mean?"

She winced. "I guess I should just say it right out loud instead of dancing around it, huh?"

"That would be good."

"So, Garrett." She made a show of clearing her throat. "Ahem. It just so happens that I am a virgin. And I can't tell you how happy it would make me if you would please be my first."

He kept his expression strictly serious. "Cami, I would be honored."

"Honored." She snickered. "I'll take it."

"But—"

She put her fingers to his lips. "Ugh. There are 'buts'?"

He smoothed her hair, a slow stroke and then another, to soothe her worried frown. "The other day, when Munch and I were eavesdropping on your private moments with the bonehead, the guy called you 'cold.'"

She gave a gusty sigh. "Yeah. Charles and I were engaged for two years and I just… I couldn't bring myself to have sex with him. I kept saying I wanted to wait—and I did. Because never would have been too soon with him, you know?"

"I get it. I met him, remember?"

"He really isn't a bad guy, Garrett."

"He tried to drag you out of here against your will. That makes him a bad guy in my book."

"Yeah, well. I still have some sympathy for him and the position he's in. I've known him all my life and I never thought of him romantically. But still, I caved and said yes to him. And then I let it get all the way to the altar before I called it off. What a disaster. I didn't have the guts to break up with him till the last possible minute, but I also refused to have my first time be with him. I can't believe what a coward I was, that it took me twenty-eight years to finally bust out on my own."

"Come on. Think positive. You're out now."

"Oh, yes, I am. And loving every minute of it, believe me."

"So I completely understand why you didn't sleep with Charles."

"Thank you."

"But what about that bad boy you ran away with in high school?"

"I told you. Robbie wasn't really bad. He was a great guy and I was sure it was true love with him. We fooled around a lot. But he was Catholic and he didn't believe in sex before marriage. So nope, not with Robbie. And you know, people make jokes about punching your V-card. But it's really not funny. The longer you're a virgin, the harder it gets to just go do it, you know? Because I never wanted to have sex with just anybody. And the years went by and I started to worry that maybe I would never have sex at all. I…I always wanted to be in love first."

In love?

Garrett's pulse kicked into overdrive and his mouth went dry. Yeah, okay. If he ever were to take a chance on love again, it would be with someone like her, someone honest and true and openhearted, someone even-tempered, who could show up on a mountain-top bloody and battered and just wave her hand and ask for water and a hot dog.

But he'd failed at love. In an epic way. His babies had died and his poor wife could never get through to him. Just the thought of going there again had his gut clenching and flop sweat breaking out on his brow. Hadn't he already made that painfully clear to her?

But then she gave him that glowing smile. "Or if not love, I wanted to find a really good friend I could trust absolutely."

He realized he'd inadvertently been holding his breath. He let it out slowly so she wouldn't notice. God, she was gorgeous. With eyes like blue agates and those lips that begged for long, wet kisses. All that, and a good heart. Integrity, too. "You're like no one I've ever known before."

"That's a good thing, right?" Her mouth trembled in the hope of a smile.

If a fairy princess married a unicorn, their first-born child would be Cami. "It's an excellent thing."

And she grinned full-out. "Whew." She scooted in closer.

He pulled up the blankets and tucked them in around her. "Now go to sleep." He switched off the light. "We have time. We don't have to rush it."

She made a tiny humphing sound. "Translation. You're turned off by the whole virgin thing."

"No. I just don't want to hurt you and I think we should take it slow."

"Oh." She didn't sound at all convinced, though he couldn't see her face to know for sure.

"Cami. Do you need me to lay it right out there for you?"

"Well, yeah. I kind of do."

"I think lube will help and I don't have any handy. I'll get some tomorrow."

"Um, okay."

"Go to sleep." He shut his eyes and willed his erection to subside.

And then she whispered, "But for tonight, what about you?"

"I'll be fine." It came out a little harsher than he meant it to.

She wasn't buying. He could almost feel her mind working. And then, finally, she asked, "It does turn you off, doesn't it? That there might be blood and I don't know what I'm doing."

"Wrong."

"I don't believe you."

A bad word escaped him. He captured her hand and brought it down between them.

"Oh!" Her fingers wrapped around him again and he made himself breathe very carefully. In. Out. In again… "Garrett, this can't be comfortable."

He nuzzled her ear. "It's been this way pretty much since you appeared on the mountain. Long showers help."

"It's just not fair."

"Don't worry about it. I'll survive."

"Stop arguing." And she kissed him.

She tasted like heaven and her hand started moving…

He sank into the kiss as she played him below. He knew he should stop her. But for a virgin, she certainly seemed to be ready for anything—and surprisingly skilled with that little hand of hers.

"Garrett," she whispered against his mouth, her hand working serious magic on his aching hardness.

And then she ducked beneath the covers.

"Cami, you don't have to…" He lost his train of thought completely as her warm, wet mouth closed around him. She kept those clever fingers good and tight at the base. "Cami… I…"

He what?

He had no idea. His brain had ceased to function. He fell back against the pillow and let her have her way with him. It didn't take long.

When he got right to the brink, he tried to warn her. "Cami, I'm going to…" Again, words deserted him.

But she just kept on driving him absolutely out of his mind.

And in the end, he surrendered completely. His

climax roared through him, emptying him out in the most perfect way.

When he could move again, he pulled her up into his arms and whispered, "You are incredible. I think I just might have to keep you in this bed indefinitely."

She sighed and settled closer.

He tucked the covers around them nice and tight. "Now will you go to sleep?" He breathed the words into her sweet-smelling hair.

"Yes, Garrett." Her lips brushed his throat.

A few minutes later, he heard her breathing even out into slumber. Not long after that, he faded off, too.

In the morning, he woke holding her close. She was curled into him, her legs tangled with his, her head tucked against his chest.

She felt really good in his arms, so womanly and soft. And she smelled of vanilla and sex. *Tonight*, he thought, they would take it all the way. He was going to make it good for her, so that when she looked back on what they'd had together, she would be glad she'd wanted him for her first.

He went off to work that day with a giant grin on his face. Nell gave him grief as usual and the drywall crew still hadn't picked up the pace. As always, even on Saturday, he had too much work to do. But he had tonight to look forward to, so for once it was easy to smile through every setback.

At a quarter of noon, Cami texted him. R U @ the office? I want to bring sandwiches.

She was fixing him lunch? Did life get any better? He texted back, @ a job site.

I can bring sandwiches wherever you are.

Grinning like an idiot, he sent her the address.

She showed up twenty minutes later wearing cut-off jeans, cowboy boots and a snug white T-shirt with Jessica Rabbit printed on the front. She'd put her yellow hair in matching high ponytails and she was about the cutest thing he'd ever seen.

The drywall guys thought so, too. They looked at her like they wanted to gobble her right up. At least they had the sense to keep their mouths shut. When her back was turned, he gave them the evil eye. They stopped staring and got to work.

Garrett took Cami out into the open area behind the house. She'd come prepared, with a basket of food and a blanket to sit on. He spread the blanket on the flattened weeds and she brought out turkey sandwiches, chips, apple wedges and bottles of iced tea.

"I've been thinking about my future," she said as she nibbled on a chip. "The first day I was here, I went into this stationery store. Great place. Art supplies, greeting cards, all kinds of gorgeous custom paper, everything. This morning I went by there again. The owner wants to sell. There's a workshop in the back. I've always wanted to set up a website, try making greeting cards using my own designs—and I could sell them on Etsy, too. If I bought the shop, I could run it and make the cards in back."

"Your eyes are shining."

Her soft cheeks flushed warm pink and she confessed, "I'm kind of excited at the idea. I would have the store to run right away and take my time with the greeting cards, kind of feel my way along, developing my own line."

He sipped his tea. "You should go for it."

"Yeah?"

He nodded. "You need money?"

"Nope. I roughed out the numbers and I'm good." She laughed. "Yes, my much-hated business degree is coming in handy, after all. And I have great credit. I'm thinking about a business loan, rather than spending any of my nest egg. Monday, I'm going to talk to my bank and see what they can do for me."

He wanted to grab her and kiss her. But if he did that, he wouldn't want to stop. And the drywall guys were probably peering out the windows to see what he and the hot blonde got up to. "We should go out tonight and celebrate."

For some reason, she hesitated to answer. Finally, she said, "Well, I haven't bought the store yet."

"Doesn't matter. I want to take you out. There's this great new place, Mirabelle's. I'll see if I can get a reservation. Seven good for you?"

She set down her sandwich and exhaled a slow breath. "Garrett, I really would love to go out to dinner with you…"

He finally got the message. She had other plans. Maybe they were good plans. Maybe she wanted to get going ASAP on finishing what they'd started last night. That would be a whole lot better than good—more like downright spectacular. His work jeans got tighter. He ordered the problem to subside and asked hopefully, "But?"

"This morning after you left…"

"Yeah?"

"Your mother called."

The issue in his pants vanished as though it had never been. He had that sinking feeling. She hadn't been angling for hours and hours of amazing sex, after all. Not even close. "What did Ma want and don't tell me you said yes?"

Blue angel eyes reproached him. "You don't have get all surly about it."

"Just tell me what she wants."

"She wants us to come to dinner at the mansion tonight—to get to know Griffin a little."

He stared at her for a long count of five before accusing, "You said yes."

She scrunched up her adorable face. "As a matter of fact, I kind of did."

When Garrett pulled the Mustang to a stop in the small parking area in front of the Bravo mansion, four other vehicles were already there. He recognized them all. His mother had summoned all five of her children.

"Everybody's here," he marveled aloud. "I can't believe nobody managed to back out."

Cami leaned across the console and tugged on the collar of his blue dress shirt. "You look so handsome." She kissed him, a light breath of a kiss that had him wanting to haul her close and kiss her some more. She wore a red wraparound dress with little white polka dots on it and he could not wait to get home and take that dress off her.

"We could just turn around and go back home," he suggested. Hey, it was worth a shot. "You could call Ma and say I suddenly felt sick."

She laughed. "Come on. It's going to be great."

"Dinner at my mother's is *never* great."

"First time for everything—come on, handsome. Let's go."

It was not great.

The invitation had been adults only. So it was Carter, Garrett, Quinn, Jody and Nell, plus wives and husbands—and Cami. Because Ma thought that Cami and Garrett were a thing.

And, come to think of it, they actually were. As of last night. More or less. In a friends-with-benefits sort of way.

In the library for cocktails, Ma made them all drink martinis, all but Jody, who was nursing her three-month-old, Marybeth.

Carter tried to refuse. "No, thanks. Got a beer?" But then his wife, Paige, whispered to him. And Carter grumbled, "Fine. A martini. Make mine a double."

Once the first round of drinks was served, Nell pulled Garrett aside. "Is this a nightmare? Tell me we're going to wake up soon."

"Griffin seems like an okay guy," he tried gamely.

Their brother Quinn, who owned a gym across the street from McKellan's, joined in. "He's in real estate in San Diego. A widower. He's got three grown children."

Jody had wandered close. She whispered, "Really, it doesn't seem like there's anything wrong with him. And the chemistry with him and Ma is pretty much off the charts."

Garrett put up a hand. "I could go my whole life without knowing that."

From over by the ornate fireplace, his mother called, "All right, you four, stop whispering in the corner and join the party."

So they went and sat with the others and talked about nothing in particular through the cocktail hour. Garrett sat next to Cami on one of the sofas and wished they were home, where he could unwrap that sexy dress and bury himself in her softness at last—but slowly, with care. Because she was a virgin and he couldn't believe she'd chosen him for her first.

He put his arm around her. She sent him a glance full of sweet, sexy promises and snuggled in a little closer. He felt like the king of the world. He breathed in her flowers and vanilla scent and loved the way that polka-dot dress wrapped in front creating an excellent view of her cleavage, which he could not wait to see more of later tonight.

Life was good. Even drinking a martini in the mansion library with his mother and her new boyfriend was almost bearable with Cami tucked up close to his side.

Griffin, who did seem to be an okay guy—aside from the fact that he was clearly doing Ma and that was just gross—told them proudly about his two daughters and his son, all three of whom were married and running the family business together. The two daughters had children.

Nell asked, "So have you met the Masters family, Ma?"

Willow sipped her martini. "I have and I love them." She *loved* them. Garrett tried to get his mind around that, Ma loving someone else's kids. She patted Griffin's knee. "It's been, what, Griff, two years since that first weekend at the Cabo house?" Griffin had already mentioned that he owned a vacation place in Cabo San Lucas. Ma gave the rest of them a cool smile. "Griff invited me and his children and grandchildren for a week to get to know each other."

"Wait a minute." Nell looked as stunned as the rest of them. "I'm just doing the math here. You met Griffin's family *two years* ago?"

Willow gave an airy sigh. "I told him I wasn't ready. But he insisted."

Griffin said quietly, "I know it's a shock to all of you. We should have told you sooner, too."

"No kidding," muttered Jody. Her husband, Seth, took her hand, a gesture clearly meant to soothe her.

Griffin seemed honestly regretful. "I wanted to meet you all long ago."

"I put him off." Willow waved a hand. "I just wasn't ready yet."

Jody cleared her throat. "How, um, long have you two known each other?"

"Five and a half years," said Griffin, eliciting more than one gasp. "We met on a Mediterranean cruise." Garrett wanted to throw his martini at the far wall. *Not even a year after Dad died. Unbelievable.* "My wife had passed away two years before." Griffin draped his arm across Willow's shoulders and she gave him an adoring smile.

"We decided to see the world together," Willow said. Garrett suppressed a snide remark. After Franklin Bravo's death, it had seemed like she was always off on some trip or other. They'd all thought she was nursing her perpetually broken heart. Should they have guessed she hadn't been traveling alone? "As friends-only, at the time," she added.

"Neither of us were looking for anything but friendship then," Griffin said.

"But slowly," said Willow, "it did become...more." Her voice was strangely soft—and warm, like her expression. It was bizarre to see her this way, so happy and relaxed. His mother was never happy and she'd always been much too watchful and calculating to actually relax.

"So much more," Griffin was saying. The two shared one of those smoldering looks that Garrett really didn't need to see. Ever.

And then his mother said, "That's why we've invited you all here this evening. Because you are my family and I love you all very much and I want you to know that I've found the man I intend to spend the rest of my life with."

"You're...getting engaged?" Nell croaked.

"We already are," Willow answered with pride.

"For the last year," added Griffin.

That brought a silence big enough to drive a tractor through.

Finally, Jody piped up weakly, "But, Ma, we had no clue."

And Nell said, as if it proved anything, "I never saw a ring. I don't see a ring now."

Willow gave Griffin yet another glowing smile. "I'm ready, darling. I'll take back my ring." And Griffin whipped out a ring with a diamond the size of Fort Knox. She offered her hand and he slid the big sparkler on her finger. "There," she said. "That's better. I admit I felt naked without it." She looked up from the giant rock to send an openly loving glance around the room. "I know. I should have told you all sooner. I should have introduced you to Griffin a long time ago. But it just felt so terribly awkward. I had always sworn that your father was the only man for me. And I realize you all view me as this sad, misguided, lonely figure who'd lost the only love of her life and could never love another. I know that I believed that myself. But then I met Griff. And slowly everything changed. I hardly knew where to begin, how to tell you that I had found someone new, someone so very special. I kept putting it off and that only made it harder. And now, finally, well, we're running out of time. We couldn't wait any longer."

"Running out of time?" demanded Carter. "Ma, are you pregnant?"

Willow let out a musical laugh. "Darling. Of course not."

"Then why?" Quinn, a former martial arts champ who wasn't afraid of anything, looked terrified.

Garrett felt pretty damn freaked himself. "Ma. What the hell are you telling us? Is somebody going to die?"

His mother laughed again, a totally un-Willow-like laugh, lighthearted and joyous. "No one's going to die, sweetheart. I meant that we're running out of time until the *wedding*. Griff and I have set the date. We're getting married in December at the Haltersham Hotel."

Chapter Nine

Cami got a little worried about Garrett during the drive home. He was too quiet. And he scowled out the windshield most of the way.

Twice, she reached over and brushed his arm. The first time he pulled out of his funk long enough to give her a smile. The second time, he caught her hand and pressed his lips to the back of it.

She appreciated the gesture. He was letting her know it wasn't her he was mad at.

But she knew that already. He was upset with Willow—really upset. Cami didn't exactly understand why.

Yeah, she got that the news of the wedding had come as a complete shock to everyone. Willow really shouldn't have waited so long to introduce the family to her new love.

But Griffin seemed like a great guy and he and Willow were obviously devoted to each other. And they had certainly known each other long enough to be confident it was the real thing.

Okay, maybe it was *too* much of a shock for Garrett. He couldn't actually be happy for his mother and her new love at this point. And the fact that Willow had sprung the wedding date on them right on the heels of the news of their engagement was a lot to take in.

She offered, "You want to talk about it?"

He turned the corner onto his street. "No, I do not."

At the house, they greeted Munchy and then Garrett let the dog out into the backyard.

He reached for her the minute he slid the glass door shut. They shared a kiss that curled her toes and made her belly hot and melty.

But when he lifted his head, his eyes were far away.

She reached up and stroked her fingers into the short hair at his temple. "Talk to me."

But he didn't. Instead, he kissed her again. His lips played on hers. She surrendered to that kiss, to the delicious taste of his mouth, to the woodsy scent of him that made her feel safe, protected and deeply desired. It thrilled her, to be wanted this way—for herself as she really was—by the wonderful man who had no plans to try and make her over into his idea of who she ought to be.

She heard a faint whining sound—Munch, wanting back in. Garrett broke the kiss to open the door. The dog bumped through and trotted to his water bowl for a noisy drink.

Garrett said, "Sorry if I'm grouchy. It's not you."

She took his hands and guided them to her hips. Then she clasped his thick shoulders. "I'll try one more time. Talk to me?"

He scanned her face as though committing it to memory. And then, at last, he said, "I wanted tonight to be perfect for you. I wanted to take you to Mirabelle's for a romantic meal, just the two of us. Instead, we had to go to the mansion and deal with Ma and the guy she hasn't bothered to mention to any of us for the past five and a half years." He touched the space between her eyebrows. "You're frowning. Why?"

"Well, I wouldn't say she hasn't bothered."

"I would."

"Garrett. She was anxious about telling you all. She didn't know how to go about it."

"Sorry. That's just no excuse."

"I think she really loves him. And that they're happy."

He glared into the middle distance for several seconds, and then, finally, he looked at her again. "I get that. I do. And the truth is, Ma annoys me no matter what she does."

"Ooo." She fluttered her eyelashes at him. "Honesty. I like it."

He reached out, eased his hand around the back of her neck and pulled her in close to him. There was no other place she would rather be. He kissed the tip of her nose. "It's just leftover crap from my childhood and I know it. And hey, she might as well be happy while she's annoying me, right?"

"Right!" Cami said it with enthusiasm. "And I had a great time. I love a good martini and the food was delicious."

He arched a thick eyebrow at her. "Not to mention the family tension you could cut with a dull, rusty knife."

"You should meet *my* parents. My mother's not so bad. But my father, well, I do love him but sometimes I wonder why. He's so sure he's right. Drives me insane."

He brushed a finger along her cheek, traced the shape of her ear and then trailed that finger down the side of her throat, stirring lovely, hot goose bumps in his wake. "Your father doesn't scare me. And I plan to go with you the first time you meet with him again."

Her heart went to mush. "You would? I have no idea why you would want to put yourself through such a thing. It's not going to be any fun."

"From what you've said about him, I don't really trust your dad. You need a friend to back you up."

A friend. Weren't they kind of beyond friendship now?

Again, she sternly reminded herself that she needed to give the guy time. Tonight was the one-week anniversary of the night that they'd met. And he was hardly like her—a love-at-first-sight kind of person.

His finger kept moving. He followed the V of her neckline, down over the curve of one breast and up the other to her collarbone, which he traced all the way out on each side and then back in, ending in the hollow at the base of her throat. "Did I tell you how much I like this dress? I like the way it clings to every perfect curve. And I really like how easy it will be to take off you." His voice had gone delightfully low and rough and his eyes had turned slumberous. His eyelashes were so beautiful, inky and thick as any girl's. "This dress really helped me to get through drinks and dinner. Every time I was tempted to say something rude to my mother, I would look at your breasts, which this dress shows off in a spectacular way, and feel better about everything." He cupped one, and she bit her lip at how good that felt. "Even the crappy things in life are more bearable when I can look at your breasts."

"You're welcome." She gazed up at him, wanting his kiss, wanting his hands all over her, wanting him inside her.

Tonight.

For her very first time.

He muttered something low and dirty. And then he grabbed her hand and led her toward the stairs and up them.

She followed eagerly, Munch at her heels.

In the master suite, he sent Munch to the corner bed. Then, right there at the door, he pulled her close and started kissing her again.

Deep kisses, dizzying. Beautiful in their intensity. Like a drug, those kisses of his. She was already addicted to them. She needed an endless supply. A lifetime of his kisses wouldn't be enough.

As he kissed her, he began taking her clothes away, untying the bow at one side of her dress, and then the little one on the inside that anchored the other side in place.

He eased it off her shoulders and it drifted to the floor. He took away her red lace bra and slipped his fingers under the tiny front of her matching thong.

Oh. My. Goodness. The things he did with those fingers of his, kissing her endlessly as he played with her, her needy moans echoing in her head before he swallowed them down. She could have come, just from that. His mouth on hers, his hand working the sweetest magic down below.

But she didn't come. Every time she would find herself rising to the peak, he would slow those perfect caresses, keeping her near the edge.

But never quite letting her fall.

"Shoes," he commanded against her lips.

She took his meaning and got rid of them, kicking one off and then the other, pushing them both out of the way with a couple of quick swipes of her bare feet.

"Bed." He bit the side of her throat and sucked on it. She would have a bruise there in the morning, a tender little testament to this magical, first-time night.

And then he scooped her up and carried her. He'd pulled back the covers earlier. She loved a man who planned ahead.

She loved *him*, with all her heart and soul.

He laid her down and made quick work of her thong, pulling it down and away in one long sweep of both hands. And then he straightened, his eyes molten gold as he gazed down at her. He began to undress, unbuttoning his shirt in quick, ruthless movements.

She gazed up at him, burning for him, her skin supersensitized, her heart throbbing slow and deep, her blood so thick and hot as it pulsed through her veins.

He dropped to the bedside chair to get rid of his shoes and socks and then he was up again, shoving his dress slacks and boxer briefs off, only slowing enough to ease them free of his erection. Such a beautiful man, broad and muscled, his thighs and arms thick and powerful, his eyes hot with promises she knew he would keep.

He pulled open the drawer by the bed and took out a condom and a little white bottle with a purple label, setting them in easy reach, his gaze holding hers the whole time.

"Cami," he said on a growl as he came down to her, a beautiful big bad wolf of a man ready to gobble her up, watching her hungrily through golden eyes. She opened her arms to him and gathered him close.

More kisses, perfect kisses. The kind that go on and on and on. It all blurred together in the best sort of way. His hands on her body, driving her higher, yet somehow never quite letting her fly over the edge. In time, his kisses strayed from her mouth. His lips brushed over her cheek and then lower, blazing trails of heat and wonder all along her eager flesh.

She cried out in pleasure, lost to him, to his burning kisses, his skilled and tender caresses. He just kept kissing her, touching her, sweeping her away on an endless wave of sweet sensation.

He rose above her on his knees. She blinked up at him, dazed and dreamy, and commanded, "Come back here."

"Oh, I will. Very soon." And he smiled at her, a sweet devil's smile, as he rolled on the condom and then used the clear gel from the little white bottle. He squirted more of the stuff on his fingers and held her gaze as he used it on her.

She moaned at his touch, at the coolness of the gel where she was burning up in the best possible way.

"You're so wet. I don't think you even need this stuff." His fingers stroked her.

"I don't care if I need it. It feels good. Cool. I like it a lot." He dipped two fingers in and she laughed in sheer delight.

"You think it's funny?" He made the question into a tender threat.

A threat of what exactly, she had no clue. "I think it's incredible—and I don't just mean the gel. I mean you and every naughty thing you do to me. I love it. All of it. As long as it's with you."

"Yeah?" Amber eyes glowed down at her.

"Yeah." She caught her lower lip between her teeth and moaned. And then those amazing fingers found a certain extrasensitive spot inside her. She let out a sharp cry at the bright bloom of increased sensation.

"Does that hurt?"

She shook her head hard and fast against the pillow. "Are you kidding? No way. It's good, really. So good…" And she moaned in need and excitement as he kept on touching her.

Her eyes were too heavy to stay open. She let them drift shut. She gave herself up to him, lifting her hips to him, opening her legs even wider, begging him with her body never to stop.

He bent closer. That soft mouth covered hers. She tasted her own desire on his lips, on his devilish tongue. So perfect, the weight of him, the heat and the hardness covering her.

And then he lifted his head away. She felt him, there, where she wanted him, nudging at her core. He pushed in so slowly.

"Oh!" She opened her eyes wide at the unaccustomed sensation.

His eyes were waiting. "Okay?" He hovered above her, inside her, but just barely.

"Very okay." She wrapped her arms loosely around his big shoulders.

"More?"

She nodded. "Yes, please."

With a slow smile, he gave her more.

It felt so good, the feeling of fullness, the unhurried, delicious stretching. She lifted her legs and wrapped them around him, too. "More," she whispered, holding his caramel gaze.

He groaned then, his brow crinkling, his beautiful mouth going softer than ever. "Cami…"

"Garrett…" She tightened her arms and legs around him, pulling him down.

Another strangled sound escaped him.

She took his face and captured his gaze. "Yes," she whispered. "I'm ready. Yes…"

"Sure?"

"Yes."

"Because, Cami, I…" That sentence died unfinished.

Not that it mattered. She answered his question again, "Yes."

And finally, he believed her. He pushed his hips toward her as she rose to take him. Her body gave to him easily, taking him in like he was born to be there.

Stillness. Total stillness in that perfect moment. Just the two of them, joined at last in the most basic way.

He braced his forearms on either side of her and pressed his forehead to hers. It was so beautiful, the feel of him inside her, the warmth of his breath across her skin. In that moment, there was only the two of them. She stared up at him, and he gazed back at her and she was glad.

So very glad, that she'd waited to have this with him.

He started to move then, slowly. He watched her as he rocked her, ready to stop if she needed that.

But stopping was the last thing she wanted or needed. She gasped at the sheer beauty of it, the hot, wet, perfect glide of him deep inside her, filling her, stretching her, stoking her pleasure. She pulled him closer, lifting herself toward him, whispering encouragements, sighing his name.

He moved faster. She wrapped herself tighter, closer, around him as they went on rising and falling, bobbing happily on their own private ocean of pleasure. She could have gone on like that forever.

But he'd played her too well and she was more than ready. And this time when she reached for the peak, he did nothing to slow her down.

The glow started, that shimmer of building sensation. The shimmer became a pool of light and the light became a rising flame. The flame spread, licking everywhere, until there wasn't an inch of her inside or out that didn't shudder and burn.

For a dazzling, perfect moment, there was nothing but light and heat filling her to overflowing as she hit the crest. A guttural, garbled sound escaped her.

And then he was pushing up onto his hands. "Cami." Those amber eyes blazed down at her as he started to move again, slow and deep at first, but pumping into her harder, faster, as he chased his own release.

He came, straining his head back, the powerful muscles in his neck standing out in sharp relief as he groaned his satisfaction out loud.

When he collapsed on top of her, she gathered him in. Even then, wrung out from his climax, he was careful not to crush her with his weight. He guided them over, so they were on their sides facing each other.

For the longest, sweetest time, they just lay there, holding each other. She never wanted to let him go.

But finally, he smoothed her hair and kissed her mouth and eased away. He settled the covers over her. "Be right back…"

She stayed where he left her, feeling weightless and wonderful, perfectly content, listening to the jingle of Munchy's collar from over in the corner and the sound of water running in the bathroom. Really, did it get any better than this?

When the bathroom door opened, she pushed back the blankets and got up. In the middle of the floor, he caught her. He smelled like soap and toothpaste and they shared a laughing kiss before he let her go to clean up a little and brush her teeth.

By the time she returned to the bedroom, Munch had reclaimed his favorite spot at the foot of the bed and Garrett had turned off the lamp. He held the covers up for her.

She slid in beside him and he pulled her back against his body, into the shelter of his strong arms.

Her father called the next day.

They were having breakfast and she made the mistake of answering without checking the display.

He started right in on her. "This is becoming ridiculous, Camilla. When are you coming home?"

"I don't want to get into it with you right now, Dad." Garrett looked up sharply from the Sunday edition of the *Justice Creek Courier*. She gave him a rueful shrug and said to her father, "As for coming to visit you, I'll let you know."

"Camilla, this is unacceptable. If you don't—"

"Talk to you later, Dad." He was sputtering in fury as she disconnected the call.

"Bad?" Garrett asked after a long, silent moment.

She gave him another shrug. "It is what it is. Do you have to work today?"

He turned the page. "You're changing the subject on me."

"That's right."

He looked at her over the top of the paper, melty brown eyes making purely sexual promises. "On occasion, I've been known to take a Sunday off."

A lovely shiver went through her. She felt beautiful and sexy and a little bit sore. But not sore enough to keep her from having the best Sunday ever. "Is this one of those Sundays?"

He set down the paper. "Finish your breakfast so we can go back to bed."

It was a beautiful day. They spent most of it in bed.

That night, he took her to Mirabelle's for a leisurely romantic dinner. And then, back at home, he carried her straight up to the bedroom again.

The next week was a busy one. She got the money from her insurance company to buy a new car. She also got a loan to buy her store and good advice on her new business venture from Garrett's half brother James, who was a partner in a small law office right there in town.

Every night, she slept wrapped in Garrett's arms. And on Monday, Tuesday and Friday, when he had no lunch meetings, she packed up the picnic basket and joined him wherever he was working that day.

The next week was just as good. Tuesday, she got a great offer on her condo and agreed to the sale. Her Realtor drove up from Denver to bring her the contract. If everything went as expected, they would close in mid-September.

That night when Garrett got home from work, she had a bottle of expensive champagne chilling on ice. They toasted the sale and then celebrated by going to bed early—and not to get extra sleep.

The next day, in his office, over roast beef on rye, they joked about how good they were for each other.

She said, "You're schooling me in Backbone 101."

That made him laugh. "You've already graduated. Look at you, getting rid of the cheating fiancé, saying no to your father no matter how much grief he tries to give you and building yourself a business that works for you."

Her plans to buy the stationery store were moving right along. She'd signed the papers two days before. By the end of the month, the old owner would be out. The deal had included all the stock, shelving, sales equipment and display units. Once the shop was hers, Cami would close for the month of September. She wanted to rearrange the place a bit, put her own stamp on it and set up her workshop in the back. Her new shop, Paper Princess, would have its gala grand opening the first Saturday in October.

In the meantime, she'd turned her bedroom at Garrett's house into a temporary workshop. For several satisfying hours a day, she sketched out her new line of Paper Princess greeting cards. She'd even fooled around with some ideas for Paper Princess paper dolls. And Chloe Bravo, Quinn's wife, had set her up with an excellent web designer. PaperPrincess.com would go live on the shop's grand opening day.

Life was good. And the man across the desk from her had a lot to do with making it that way.

Cami sipped her iced tea and grinned. "Backbone 101 isn't all you've helped me with." She granted him a wicked grin. "There's also my sex education."

"Watch it," he warned in a growl. "I'll be forced to hold a special class. Right here on this desk."

Sex in his office? In the middle of the day? Heat bloomed in her belly. "I'm a big supporter of continuing education."

He waved the last of his sandwich at her. "Finish your lunch and prepare to get schooled."

"Yes, Professor." She made a show of batting her eyelashes at him. "And if *you're* teaching *me* about the endless joy of sex and the deep satisfaction of standing up to my controlling father, what am *I* teaching *you*?"

He ate the last bite of watermelon from the fruit cup she'd packed for him. "Hmm. Maybe, how to take time off now and then? The health benefits of sharing lunch with someone hot and fun and sexy? How to deal with my mother and not want to kill her?"

Cami blushed with happy pleasure. She did love

this man and she longed to tell him so. Too bad she couldn't shake the feeling that he wasn't ready to hear it yet. "So then, Health and Life Skills. A guy needs those, right?"

"Absolutely, he does." He balled up the plastic wrap from his sandwich and lobbed it at the trash can. Then he swung his boots to the floor, stepped to the door and twisted the lock. "And now for a little higher education…"

Cami left Garrett's office that day with an extra-wide smile on her face.

Unfortunately, half an hour later, as she was playing fetch with Munchy in Garrett's backyard, her father called again. That time, she had sense enough to check the display before answering.

She let it go to voice mail and took Munch inside, where she got to work on her greeting cards. Time passed in a happy creative haze. She came up with several new card designs and cute text to go with them.

At a little after five, she knocked off. It was Garrett's turn to deal with dinner so she didn't have to figure out what do about the meal that night.

Munchy always liked a walk. He danced around in circles when he saw her get his leash.

"Sit." Quivering with happiness, he dropped to his haunches. She praised him as she hooked the leash to his collar.

They had a nice two-mile stroll. The whole way she thought about the voice mail she hadn't listened to yet.

Guilt was making her stomach knot up, so when they got back to the house, she listened to her father's message—and couldn't resist talking back to his re-corded voice as he listed her sins.

"Camilla." He let out a sigh that came through loud and clear, even in voice mail. "I'm at the end of my rope here. I don't know what to do about you."

"How 'bout this, Dad?" she scoffed at the phone. "Try respecting my choices and allowing me to live my own life."

"You've hurt me deeply and broken your poor mother's heart."

She moaned. "Oh, come on."

"And what about Charles? The man carries on, but all his joy in life is gone."

"Joy? I stole his joy?" She almost threw her poor phone at the wall about then. "I don't remember him having a lot of that in the first place."

"If you won't take my calls, at least call your mother. She hasn't smiled since you vanished from your own wedding."

"Great, Dad. Thanks. Now it's all my fault if Mom is unhappy."

"I mean it, Camilla. This has gone on long enough. Stop being a spineless coward. Come to dinner at least. Let's talk this over like reasonable adults."

That night, Garrett brought takeout from Romano's restaurant. Italian from Romano's was her favorite, but Cami hardly gave the take-out bags a glance.

"What's the matter?" he asked.

"It's nothing. Let's eat."

She'd already set the table. He petted his dog, washed his hands and they sat down to dinner.

"Ma called today," he said, hoping that might rouse

her out of her uncharacteristic funk. Cami loved to hear news about Ma and Griffin.

"She and Griffin are still in town?"

"They're living here until December. She said they would go back to California for Labor Day and also for a week in October. His family's coming here for the wedding. They'll all stay at the mansion for a week. After the wedding, Ma's moving to Southern California—but she and Griffin will be coming back to visit often, she said." He watched Cami take a tiny sip of wine and tear a piece of bread in half. "But here's the big news…"

Cami glanced up from the food she wasn't eating. "What?"

"Ma wants to deed the mansion to Sondra's children."

That seemed to perk her up a little. "Wow."

"And not only the mansion. She wants to give Sondra's kids the antiques and pricey furniture that used to belong to their mom. Ma said she thought it was the right thing to do. Can you believe it, Ma wanting to do the right thing by Dad's first wife's children? Pigs are flying, I kid you not."

Across the table, Cami managed a chuckle at least. "You know, I do like your mom."

"I've been meaning to ask you why."

"Oh, come on. You know why. She's smart. And she's perceptive. She has a sense for what's really going on with people."

"I find her seriously self-absorbed."

"Stop." She faked a glare. But then the smile returned, slightly dreamy this time. "Plus, she and Griffin? I have to tell you, it's beautiful to see them together. They're living proof that love can find you even when you think romance and passion are long gone from your life."

"Can you not talk about passion and my mother in the same sentence, please?"

She pointed her fork at him. "You are such a prude."

"You weren't calling me a prude all spread out on my desk today."

"Well, okay," she relented, a tiny smile playing at the corner of her mouth. "You're only a prude when it comes to your mother."

As if there was something wrong with that. "You bet I am."

Cami let out a little snort of derision. "And another great thing about your mom? She makes a mean martini."

"She ought to. She's had enough practice." He launched into the rest of his story. "So anyway, Ma said she was calling all of us—her own children, I mean—to see what we thought of her giving the house to Sondra's kids. I said go for it. Nell did, too. Nell and I are a hundred percent positive that Carter, Quinn and Jody will feel the same. Nobody but Ma and Dad ever thought it was okay for him to just move Ma into the house he built for Sondra, especially when the poor woman hadn't been dead a week." He shook his head. "There's been a lot of bitterness over that house. I think all the bad feelings are gone now, but for Ma to give it back to Sondra's children…" He sipped his beer. "Yeah. It's the right thing."

Cami pushed her veal around on her plate. "You

think one of your half brothers or -sisters will want to live there now?"

"Doubtful. Maybe Clara or Elise will want the place. But it's not likely. They'll probably end up selling it. I warned Ma of that, even though I expected my saying it would piss her off."

"But it didn't."

Sometimes he wondered if Cami knew his mother better than he did. "Not in the least. Ma says if they want to sell it all and split the proceeds, that's up to them. And Estrella, the mansion's longtime housekeeper, is ready to retire, so she won't be put out of a job."

Cami raised her wineglass. "Way to go, Willow." Garrett raised his beer, reaching across to tap her glass with it. They both drank.

And then she went right back to fiddling with her food.

He'd had enough of watching her be miserable. "Do you think maybe it's time to tell me what's wrong?" When she only glanced up glumly, he added, "That's veal piccata, in case you didn't notice. Veal piccata from Romano's and you've hardly had a bite. It's a sin before God and his angels not to eat every bite of a dinner that comes from Romano's."

"You're right. Sorry." She cut a tiny wedge of the tender veal and ate it. "It's amazing. Thank you."

He set down his fork. "Look. Whatever's got you so down, I want to know about it. Will you please talk to me?"

She wiped her mouth with her napkin, which was totally unnecessary, given that she'd hardly eaten anything. "Did you mean what you said about going with me the first time I went to see my parents?"

"You know I did. Anytime, anyplace. I'm going with you."

"You're the best. I mean that. I should remember that I'm supposed to be getting an A in Backbone 101 and insist that I don't need you there. But really, I do."

"I'm there. So then, you talked to them?"

"My dad called this afternoon. I didn't answer, but I played his voice mail a few hours later. He said a bunch of mean crap. But he was right that I need to go and see them. It's been almost a month since I left."

Almost a month…

How could that be? It seemed like just yesterday that she'd appeared at the cabin.

And yet, at the same time, he felt that he'd known her all his life, that he knew every inch of her, inside and out.

Imagining a day without her in it? He couldn't. She filled up all the spaces in his world that he hadn't even realized were empty, filled them with her happy laugh and her wide blue eyes and her body that thrilled him and also somehow felt like home.

He wanted her with him, bringing him lunch in a basket, offering herself for dessert. It was way beyond friendship and that freaked him out a little—okay, fine. It freaked him out a lot.

And what about the prospect of losing her when she decided it was time to strike out on her own? It caused a physical ache in him to even consider her leaving, to imagine his bed without her in it, her seat at his table empty.

But where else was this thing with them going to

go? It wasn't forever or anything. She'd barely gotten rid of the bonehead. No way was she ready to get serious again.

That made him…what to her?

A rebound guy, that was what. Best case, he could consider himself a temporary hero at a time when she needed one. They were friends with some serious benefits going on.

He needed to quell all these feelings he wasn't even supposed to be having and live in the damn moment.

She was watching him way too closely. "You okay, Garrett?"

"Fine." He needed to get off the emo train immediately. The whole point was that he hated all the emotional back-and-forth that happened in a serious relationship—not to mention, he sucked at it.

Which was why he didn't *have* serious relationships.

Never again.

He needed to focus on loving every minute with her, on being there for her as long as that worked for her. When the day came that she was ready to strike out on her own, he wouldn't hold her back.

And what were they talking about, anyway?

Right. Her dad. "So then, you went ahead and called him?"

"Yeah."

"And?"

"He said more mean things to me. The usual ones. I'm flighty and irresponsible and I need to cut that out immediately and do things the way he wants them done—meaning the *right* way. Which is to say, *his* way."

"Cami. Is there a downstroke here?"

Her smooth brow puckered. "A downstroke?"

"I mean, I completely get that your dad's an over-bearing jerkass. But are we going to Denver anytime soon?"

"You really don't have to go with—"

"Yeah, I do. I want to. Are we going or not?"

She puffed out her cheeks on a big exhale. And then finally, she gave it up. "Saturday night at seven. Dinner at my parents' house."

Chapter Ten

From outside, Garrett eyeballed the Lockwood house at around ten thousand square feet. It sat on a slight hill in superexclusive North Cherry Creek and had two stories aboveground. Judging by the windows that gleamed below ground level, the house also included a fully finished basement.

Cami's father answered the doorbell. Quentin Lockwood was tall and very lean with a long face etched in what appeared to be a permanent scowl. Cami must have gotten her looks from her mom.

"Camilla." Lockwood's scowl deepened at the sight of Garrett. "Hello."

"Hello, Dad." Cami's voice was so cautious, so over-controlled. Garrett's exasperation with her father ratcheted up several notches. Anyone who dimmed Cami's joy and enthusiasm was a dirtball in Garrett's book.

Lockwood stepped back. "Come in."

They crossed the threshold. The soaring entry had two stories of curved windows on either side of the coffered front door.

Lockwood's surly silence and hostile staring were interrupted by a gorgeous blue-eyed blonde. She fluttered in from the next room, slim arms outstretched. "Oh, sweetheart. Here you are."

"Mom." Cami stepped forward and the two women embraced.

"At last." With a happy sigh, Hazel Lockwood pressed Cami close. "I'm so glad you came." Cami's mom seemed sincere at least. And she actually sent Garrett a welcoming smile over Cami's shoulder.

When the women pulled apart, Cami embraced her father stiffly and then took Garrett's left arm. "Mom, Dad. This is Garrett Bravo." Her face lit up with a mischievous smile. "Garrett is my *special* friend."

Her mother greeted him warmly. "It's so nice to meet you, Garrett."

And her father finally offered his hand. Garrett shook it and then Lockwood said, "Well, all right, then. Shall we go on into the library for drinks?"

Cami gave Garrett's arm a squeeze. "Just like at the mansion, huh?"

"Excuse me?" said her father.

Garrett explained, "My mother always serves drinks in the library."

"I hope you'll feel right at home, then," Lockwood replied sourly. "This way." He ushered them through a wide arch into a two-story room finished in way too much glossy, deep red Brazilian cherry. There was a parquet cherry floor, a looming fireplace with a cherry surround, cherry platform steps on three walls leading up to glassed-in cherry bookcases full of leather-bound volumes. The gracefully curving cherry staircase climbed one wall to a second-floor gallery railed in cherry.

A fat sofa with too many pillows, an ornate coffee table and three large armchairs cozied up to the unlit fireplace. Garrett and Cami took the couch. Quentin offered drinks. He whipped them up while Hazel urged them to help themselves to the giant tray of different cheeses and gourmet crackers waiting on the coffee table.

Once they all had drinks, Lockwood folded his long frame into a studded leather throne of a chair and said, "Camilla, it is wonderful to see you." At Cami's careful nod and strained smile, he added reproachfully, "Though it was my understanding you would be coming alone."

Cami's tight smile died a sudden death. "The way I remember it, you *wanted* me to come alone, but I told you that I planned to bring Garrett if he could make it."

Hazel piped up with, "Honey, we're glad you brought your friend with you." Lockwood started to speak, but she beat him to it. "Now, tell us how you've been doing. How are things in Justice Creek?"

"I love it there." Cami slid closer to Garrett. Her fingers brushed his thigh, seeking contact. He caught them and held on. She launched into a quick recap of her progress in the past month, how she'd gotten to know so many people, had begun volunteering in the community. "I work a few afternoons a week helping out at the animal shelter and I've agreed to help

a Blueberry troop make their own Christmas cards."
She told them about Paper Princess. "Greeting cards
and stationery. My store opens in October. I hope
you'll come to my grand opening."

"Expressing your creative side, right?" Hazel beamed.
"We would love to come. Wouldn't we, Quentin?"

Lockwood ignored his wife. "We need you back at
WellWay. And you could at least give Charles a call.
He's having a hard time without you."

"Dad." Cami sounded weary now. "Where to even
begin with you? I'll say it all again. I'm not coming
back to—"

"Don't," commanded Lockwood. "Please."

"You know what? You're right. I've said it too
many times. And I know you've heard me, so that's
that. We can just let it be."

Hazel chirped, "Are you sure you wouldn't like
some cheese?"

"Mom." Cami shook her head. "Forget the cheese."

"What is that you're wearing?" asked Lockwood,
eyeing Cami's yellow sundress. She looked like a million bucks in that dress. It had skinny little shoulder
straps, laces up the back and the hem went every
which way, like a bunch of yellow handkerchiefs sewn
together. "It's not your style at all."

"Wrong," said Cami flatly. "This dress is exactly
my style."

Garrett agreed. And he said so. "It's perfect on
you. *You're* perfect." Was he laying it on too thick?
Not a chance. Lockwood needed to have his eyes ex-
amined if he thought there was anything wrong with
that dress or the woman wearing it.

Lockwood knocked back a slug of scotch. "I do

not understand you, Camilla. I really thought you'd finally settled down and come to realize—"

"Well, Dad. I did come to realize a few things, now you mention it, though they are actually things I've always known. That I want a different life than you had planned for me, that I was never going to be happy trying to be who you wanted me to be."

"Happy." He repeated the word with a sneer.

"Yeah." She came right back at him. "Happy. Because happiness matters. It's even in the Declaration of Independence, in case you might have forgotten. Everybody's entitled to 'life, liberty and the pursuit of happiness.' Well, I had a life, all right. But it wasn't much without the *liberty* to decide how I wanted to live it. And there was no way I could pursue my own *happiness* with a man I didn't love and a job that made me want to run away screaming."

Garrett almost applauded. The woman was magnificent. She really didn't need him here, but he was kind of glad she'd brought him along. It was seriously enlightening to witness firsthand what a self-righteous ass her father was.

She finished with, "And if we're just going to sit here and cover the same ground over and over again, I think Garrett and I should just give up and go." She started to stand.

But her mother cried, "No. Please don't go, honey." Hazel turned reproachful eyes on Lockwood. "Quentin." This time, her voice actually held a note of steel beneath the sweetness.

Lockwood answered with a bitter edge. "All right. I'll keep my mouth shut. You don't want to hear it and I'm tired of saying it."

"Please stay," Hazel pleaded.

Garrett was more than ready to get the hell out. But this was Cami's show.

Finally, Cami nodded. "I guess we can give it a try."

So they stayed. They finished their drinks and went in to dinner, which was served in a formal dining room by a middle-aged woman in black.

Hazel tried to keep the conversation going. She asked Garrett about his work and got Cami talking about her shop some more. Mostly, though, the meal consisted of long stretches of painful silence punctuated by the clink of monogrammed silverware against fine china plates.

Lockwood hardly said a word through the meal, but his reserve was far from benign. He reminded Garrett of a long, skinny tiger crouched to strike.

Mostly though, Cami's father behaved himself. There were plenty of snide remarks and way too much scowling, but at least he was reasonably civil and the evening limped along.

The woman in black served coffee and dessert. Garrett dared to hope they would get through the final course and get the hell out before anything too awful happened.

But ultimately, Quentin Lockwood just couldn't leave bad enough alone.

Garrett had taken only one bite of his tiramisu when Cami's dad brought out the big guns. "Hazel," he said severely. "I'm sorry if I'm about to upset you, but there comes a time when a man is finally forced to draw the line."

"Quentin, I mean it." Hazel spoke fervently. "Don't you dare." Her mouth was trembling.

Cami set down her spoon. "Is this a threat of some kind, then?"

Lockwood said, "It's your last chance, that's what it is."

"Dad, I thought we already—"

He ran right over her. "I want you to return to Denver and take your rightful place at WellWay again. I don't know if Charles will be willing to take you back at this point, but I insist that you at least try to patch things up with him."

"Is that all?" Cami asked.

"Not quite. I want you to go back into therapy, where you will examine why you feel compelled to keep walking out on your own life. And I want your sincere promise that you will never run away again."

Cami just stared at him for several unnerving seconds, after which she replied quietly, "No."

Lockwood actually seemed kind of surprised. The guy refused to believe that Cami wouldn't finally cave to his will. "No, to…?"

"All of it, Dad—well, except for promising never to run away again. I can make that promise now because I'm finally where I want to be."

The frown lines in Lockwood's forehead got deeper than ever. "Meaning…?"

"That I live in Justice Creek now, and as I've said repeatedly, I love it there."

"Well, all right, then, Camilla." For the first time that evening, the man smiled. It wasn't a pretty sight. He raised his delicate china coffee cup as though to make a toast and announced, "I am disowning you."

Hazel gasped. From the expression on her pretty face, she'd had no idea her husband would go that far.

But Cami didn't even flinch. "*Disown.* See, that's the problem, Dad. You never *owned* me in the first place."

"Don't give me your clever wordplay. You know what I mean. You will get nothing. I'll cut you out of our wills, out of WellWay, out of all of it."

That single bite of tiramisu seemed stuck in Garrett's throat. And here he'd thought the Bravos had issues. "Cami." When she looked at him, he tipped his head in the direction of the front door.

She gave him the saddest little smile. "Not yet, Garrett." She turned her calm gaze on her father. "What else, Dad?"

"You think I'm bluffing?" Lockwood taunted. "I'm not bluffing."

"Quentin." Hazel's voice was hardly more than a desperate whisper this time.

He ignored her. "Sadly, Camilla, I don't know what else to do about you. You are a confused and pathetic creature who doesn't know how to run her own life, a woman who is clearly a danger to herself. Over and over, you have taken the wrong turns, made the self-defeating choices. Every time your mother and I become confident you've finally taken your rightful place in the world, you run off on some wild-goose chase again. Well, this it. You're out on your ear and I refuse to feel guilty about cutting you loose. I'm hardly leaving you destitute. You got your trust fund. Take care of the money you already have. Because the real family fortune will never be yours."

Cami said nothing. She sat very still. Even with

that stricken look on her face, she was a bright ray of sunshine in her yellow dress.

But Garrett couldn't sit still. He'd heard way more than enough. He shoved back his chair and dropped his napkin on the table. "We're outta here."

Cami stayed in her chair. "I'm sorry you had to see this, Garrett. But I'm not leaving. Not yet. Not until I've had my say."

I'm here for backup, he reminded himself. *It's her fight, not mine.* Slowly, he sank back to his seat.

Cami turned to her father. "I love you, Dad." She spoke gently, with real kindness. "I can't be what you want. If I could, I would have changed myself long before now. But I'm just…not that person. Not the Lockwood you always wanted me to be. I'm sorry. I really am. But you go ahead and do what you have to do. In the meantime, I'm going to be happy in Justice Creek, doing work I love with people I care about who feel the same for me. And I truly hope that someday you'll miss me and decide that maybe it's time you gave up trying to run my life, time to let yourself just love me as I love you. Until then, well…" She slid her napkin in beside her plate and silently pushed back her chair.

Garrett stood again and went to her side.

She took his hand and said to her father, "The sad thing is, there was a time when your threats would have worked on me. But that time is past, Dad. I won't stop hoping, though, that someday you'll find a way to accept that I finally grew up and became who I really am."

Her father threw up both hands. "All that's just nonsense. *Who you really are.* What does that even mean? I am done with—"

"Stop!" Hazel Lockwood shouted. Shocked the hell out of Garrett—and Cami and her dad, too, judging by the stunned looks on their faces. Hazel shoved back her chair and popped to her feet. "I've had about enough of this, Quentin." Cami clutched Garrett's hand tighter as Hazel rounded on her husband. "This can't go on. Cami's right. And you are wrong, my love. She's a grown woman and she has a right to make her own choices." She marched down the long table to loom above him. "Take it back," she demanded. "Apologize this instant."

Was this really happening? Garrett slid a glance at Cami. She looked as astonished as he felt. He'd spent a grim two hours with the Lockwoods. It was long enough for him to feel certain that Cami's mom had never been the kind of woman to call out her man.

Until now, anyway.

About then, Quentin got past his stupefaction that his wife had dared to stand up to him. "Hazel, what is the matter with you? I don't believe this."

She fisted her hands at her sides and insisted, "Take it back, Quentin. Take it back now."

"That does it." He jumped up. "I've said what I had to say. Camilla, do not come back. I've had more than enough of your foolish self-destructive behaviors. Good night, everyone."

And with that, he stormed from the room.

At the door, Cami hugged her mother. "Thanks for trying, Mom."

"I'll have a long talk with him. It will work out, you wait and see." Hazel's anxious eyes belied her words. "Garrett, it was lovely to meet you."

"Thanks, Mrs. Lockwood."

"Hazel. Please." She opened the door and they went down the wide stone steps and got into the Mustang.

When Garrett started up the engine and pulled away, Hazel lifted a hand in a wave.

"You doing okay over there?" he asked when they were out on the highway speeding toward home. Forty-five minutes had passed without Cami saying a word.

"I'm sad." She stared out the windshield as the dark highway fled past behind them.

"You're amazing."

"Yeah?" she asked hopefully, but she didn't look at him. Her eyes remained on the road ahead.

"Are you kidding me? Look at you. You've accomplished everything you set out to do, made a life in Justice Creek on your own terms. You've faced down your overbearing ex-fiancé and your controlling dad. No question about it. You blow me away."

Did she almost smile? He wasn't sure. She stared out at the night and said somberly, "I love my dad. He's not always a complete jerk. When I was little, he used to give me piggyback rides and play catch with me. He always treated Mom like his queen and me like a princess. I won a prize in an art show once. He was so proud. It's just, you know, I'm his only kid and he had plans for his kid." She turned to look at him then. "But I'm not going back. No way." She leaned across the console and put that fine mouth close to his ear. Her breath warmed his skin. "Thanks for coming with me."

He turned to claim a quick, sweet kiss. "What's a friend for?"

Something happened in those big blue eyes—a withdrawal, maybe? Or maybe not, because a moment later, she put a finger to his chin and turned his face her way again for another swift and tempting kiss. A low, sexy laugh escaped her. "Take me home, handsome. I want to show you what a good friend I am."

"That is by far the best offer I've had all night." He turned his eyes to the road and drove a little faster, inching it over the speed limit, eager to undo the laces of that yellow dress and explore their *special* friendship in a mutually satisfying way.

"Cami?" She heard the cautious tap of Garrett's knuckles against the bathroom door.

"Be right out." She stared at her reflection in the mirror above the sink. In a strapless bra of ivory lace and matching thong, she was all ready for seduction.

Except for the sadness that she couldn't seem to shake.

Because her dad had just kicked her out of his life.

And the man she loved kept calling her his *friend*.

Yeah, okay. That wasn't fair to Garrett. He'd taken care of her on the mountain, opened his home to her, introduced her to his friends and family, backed her up when anything threatened her. And shown her how glorious lovemaking could be. She had no right to expect him to fall in love with her just because she'd fallen for him.

Why *shouldn't* Garrett call her a friend? She *was* a friend. And if she wanted more from him than friendship and amazing sex, she had to put herself out there, to tell him what she felt in her heart.

That was the first step, after all. She needed to say, *I love you, Garrett,* and give the guy a chance to respond.

"You okay?" He was still there, waiting for her on the other side of the door.

Squaring her shoulders, she went and opened the door to him. "I'm perfect," she lied.

"Oh, yes, you are." He wore absolutely nothing and he looked spectacular that way. His eyes full of sexy promises, he reached out and touched her shoulder. "Turn around."

She obeyed, showing him her back. His clever fingers got to work. Her bra fell away. She caught it before it dropped to the floor. His fingers skated along the length of her arm, stirring hot little flares of pleasured sensation. He took the bra from her fingers. She didn't look to see what he did with it.

His warm palm glided around to cup her bare breast. He pulled her back against his chest and she went with a willing sigh, letting her head fall onto his shoulder, feeling his heat and hardness pressing into the cleft of her bottom, the head notching against the small of her back.

She whispered his name, "Garrett," in arousal and longing. In sadness and gratitude.

And most of all, in love.

He wrapped his hand around her throat, claiming it, claiming *her*, all of her, body, soul and yearning heart. She shuddered in pleasure, letting him guide her, tipping her head all the way back until their lips could meet.

A long kiss, wet and deep and thrilling. He trailed his hand down the front of her to cup her breast again and tease the nipple, but only for a moment. His fingers drifted on downward to the sensitive terrain of her belly. She moaned into the kiss as his fingers slipped beneath the barely there cover of her thong and found her waiting heat.

She cried things, desperate things, "Please," and, "More," and, "Never, ever stop," as those wonderful fingers of his played her like a song. All the while, he kept on kissing her, until her knees gave out and she came with a shouted, "Yes!"

And then he scooped her up high in his arms and carried her to the bed. He took away her thong and they were both completely naked.

My love, she thought, staring up into those amber eyes. *I love you so.*

But she didn't say it. She feared he wouldn't want to hear it. And she'd had more than enough sadness for one night. Instead, she reached for him and opened her body to him the way she longed to open her soul.

Much later, in the dark, as he slept beside her and Munchy lay curled up at the foot of the bed, she let the sadness wash over her. For the father who considered it his right to try to force her to be someone she didn't want to be.

And for her own cowardice in the face of love.

By Wednesday of that week, Garrett knew something wasn't right with Cami—something that had nothing do with the cruel thing her father had done.

How many times now had he glanced her way to find her watching him? And then, just when he would think she was going to say something important, she would look away.

He knew he should ask her what was going on.

But he didn't ask. He really wasn't all that sure he wanted to know.

On Thursday, he came home at seven to find her in the kitchen staring out the window over the sink. It was her turn to come up with dinner, but there was nothing cooking. She usually set the table. Not tonight.

She must have heard him come in through the living room, but she didn't acknowledge him. She just stood there and stared out at the thick lower branches of the Douglas fir in the side yard.

Munch wiggled over to greet him. He crouched to give the dog some love.

When he stood up again, she turned to face him. "Hey." She leaned back against the counter, her bare feet with their cute turquoise-painted toes shuffling against the hardwood floor.

Was she nervous? She kind of seemed like it.

"I'm guessing we're going out?" he asked. "How about the Sylvan Inn? I've been meaning to take you there. It's cozy and the hammer steaks and cheesy potatoes will rock your world."

Her smooth throat clutched as she swallowed. "Could we, um, sit down for a minute? I need to talk."

What about? What's going on? "Sure."

She put out a hand. "The living room, maybe?"

Now *he* was the one gulping. They stared at each other. He had that feeling again—that whatever she had to say, he didn't want to hear it.

But he followed obediently when she turned for the other room.

She dropped to one end of the sofa, curling her legs to the side and facing him.

He took the other end. "So what's this about?"

She folded her hands on her thigh, then unfolded them and stretched out an arm along the back of the sofa. "I'm just going to say it." She brought her arm down and clasped her hands again. And then she stared down at them as though she wondered how they got there on the ends of her arms.

Had something happened with her father or the bonehead? "Cami. *What?*"

And she looked up into his eyes. "Garrett. I just have to tell you. I'm in love with you. I've been in love with you since the first moment I saw you and I don't care if that's impossible, that's how it is for me. I love you. I want to be with you. I…want more than friendship with you. More than *benefits*. Garrett, I love you and I want *everything* with you."

Love.

A rough symphony of bad words played through his mind. His throat ached and the inside of his mouth felt like he'd just tried to eat a bucket of sand. She sat there with her misplaced hands, looking like an angel in blue jeans with turquoise toes.

He wanted her. More than anything. Wanted just what they had, nights wrapped around each other and lunch in a basket. Her laughter, her soft voice, her vanilla scent, those otherworldly eyes.

But love?

No. Uh-uh.

If only she hadn't said it. If only she could have

just left it alone. He didn't want to dig down into the love place. He'd been there and done that and didn't have what love took.

Uh-uh. Not doing that again.

And still, she kept looking at him, kept waiting for him to say something, to tell her what he *felt* for her, to say she was everything and he couldn't live without her, that yes, he loved her, too.

This was it. This was where he disappointed her. This was the thing he didn't really know how to do. "Cami, I...just don't know what to say."

She caught her lower lip between her teeth and looked down at her hands again. "I meant to be patient," she said in a whisper. "But I guess I'm just not the patient type. Not anymore." Her bright head came up and she looked at him, seeking something she wasn't going to find.

For way too long, they just stared at each other.

And finally, she spoke again. "I can't thank you enough for all you've done for me. You've been the best friend I've ever had. And I still want your friendship, Garrett." That didn't sound so bad. He almost let himself breathe again. But then she said, "Eventually, I hope we can be friends again."

That pissed him off. *"Again?"* He practically shouted the word. She flinched and he made himself lower his voice. "But we *are* friends. Right now. I *want* what we have." His voice got louder again. He forced it down. "I don't want to lose you."

She held out her hands, palms up, fingers wide. And then she gathered them in to rest, one over the other, in the center of her chest. "It hurts too much. I have…all this longing. For you. For your love. Right now, for me, our friendship just isn't enough."

"You can't just—"

"Yeah. Yeah, I can. I *have* to. I love you. And to be here with you when my love is just burning inside me, when all I can think about is giving that love to you and having you give it back to me from your heart…" She shook her head. "Something has to change in me. I need to find my patience again, to be willing to wait for you, hoping someday you'll be able to openly return my love. Or if not that, then I need to somehow come to accept that you're never really going to be mine. But for now, until something changes, I can't be your friend and I can't live here with you anymore."

What? She was leaving? Just like that? His heart thudded so loud his ears were ringing. His mouth tasted bitter and his skin had shrunk so he felt stuffed tight inside it. "That's wrong. That's ridiculous. Of course you can live here. I *want* you here. I don't want you to go."

"But I have to go."

"No, you don't."

"Yeah. It's time. I need to get my own place."

He strove for calm, for a reasonable approach. "I… Look. Let's go get something to eat." He rose. "And then you can sleep on it. No big decisions have to be made right this minute."

She unfolded those shapely legs and stood to face him. "Garrett." She gazed at him with tender sadness. "I've made my decision. I know what I have to do. I'm going to pack up my stuff and get out of here tonight."

"But…where are you going to go at seven-thirty on Wednesday night?"

"It's not a big deal. I'll get a hotel room. I've always wanted to stay at the Haltersham. I think I'll try there." She reached out as if to reassure him somehow—but then she let her hand drop to her side without touching him. "I will be fine." And just like that, she turned and walked away.

Chapter Eleven

He didn't know how to stop her, so he just stood there like a brain-dead fool as she headed for the stairs.

And then he couldn't bear it.

He wasn't going to be able to watch her go, so he got his dog and left in the Wrangler. He ate fast food from a drive-through, then went to his office. He left the Jeep in the parking lot and took Munch for a long walk up one side of Glacier Avenue and back down the other.

When he returned to Bravo Construction, it was a quarter of nine. Was she gone yet?

And had she needed his help carrying her stuff out to the car?

Well, so what if she'd needed him? He wasn't about to help her leave him. She would have to do that on her own.

Just in case she was still at the house, he went on into the deserted office. He made coffee and drank too much of it and signed the stack of payables Shelly had left on his desk. There was always plenty to do at BC. He spent a couple more hours plowing through paperwork.

Every time he made the mistake of glancing at his dog, Munch would stare up at him reproachfully, as if the damn dog already knew that Cami had left and it was all Garrett's fault.

Around one in the morning, he took Munch for a quick walk around the parking lot. Then he went back inside and stretched out on his office couch.

When he woke up, it was six in the morning. He and Munch returned home.

Inside, he found her keys on the kitchen counter with a scratch-paper note. She'd drawn one of her bunny characters, the girl bunny in a ballerina skirt with a pink bow between her bunny ears. The bunny wore a sad expression. She sat in a patch of grass dotted with wildflowers and waved her bunny paw at him. Beneath the sketch, Cami had written, *I got a room at the Haltersham. I will be fine. Please take care of yourself and give Munchy a big hug for me.*

Garrett went through the motions of starting his day. He fed the dog and gave him fresh water. He ate some breakfast and took a shower.

He and Munch were back at the office at a little after eight.

Somehow, he got through the day, though Nell asked him what was wrong about ten times, and each time, he lied and said there was nothing.

Lunch was bad. He didn't have a lunch meeting. Shelly ordered him takeout. He ate at his desk and tried not to picture Cami sitting in the guest chair, nibbling on apple wedges, laughing at something he'd said.

He worked late, ate at the Sylvan Inn by himself and got home at ten. That night, he crashed in one of the spare rooms. No way he could face his empty bed yet.

Friday, he got to work before eight.

Nell was waiting for him. "I want to talk to you." She followed him into his office and slammed the door so hard it hurt his head.

He put his hand to his ear. "Easy, Nellie. You'll knock that door off its hinges."

His baby sister folded her arms across her Bravo Construction T-shirt and gave him the evil eye. "What did you do to Cami?"

Alarm rang through him. "What happened? Is she okay?"

"No thanks to you. Ma, Griffin and Elise were at the Haltersham yesterday afternoon hammering out wedding plans." Their half sister Elise was a caterer and wedding planner.

"Ma's having Elise plan the wedding?"

"Elise is the best. Everybody knows it. And she's all excited that Ma would ask her—and Elise doing Ma and Griff's wedding is not what I'm talking about."

He dropped to his desk chair. "Cami." Just saying her name made his bones ache with longing.

"Yeah, you idiot. Cami. Ma spotted her in the Haltersham lobby and asked her what was going on, why was she there? She said she was staying at the hotel until she found a place of her own. You know Ma.

She got right on it, asking what was up between you two. Cami wouldn't talk about it. Ma said no way she was letting Cami stay at a hotel. If she needed a place, she could stay at the mansion. Cami thanked her but refused. Ma called me. I was finishing up at the job site, so I went right over there."

He didn't need a blow-by-blow. "So what you're telling me is that Cami's all right?"

"She wouldn't say it, but I know what you did. You broke her heart, you big jerk. If I didn't love you, I'd slap you silly about now."

"Lay off me, Nell. It's bad enough without you riding my ass."

At least that shut her up. For about thirty seconds. And her voice was marginally softer when she said, "Anyway, I convinced her to take the spare room up at my place until she finds something."

"That's good." She would be with family. It eased his mind a little.

And then whatever mental peace he'd found shattered all to hell when his sister said, "Ma wants to see you."

That wasn't happening anytime soon. "Ma can wait."

Nell made a snorting sound before adding, "Also, Cami's dad called her last night while she was getting settled in at the loft."

His gut clenched. "Can't that SOB just leave her alone?"

"Relax. It's a good thing. Her dad apologized. For everything. Evidently, her mother walked out on him. It was a come-to-Jesus moment for Cami's dad. He and her mom are back together already and he swore to Cami's mom that he would make things right, that he would give up trying to get Cami to live her life by his rules."

"So then, Cami's no longer disowned and disinherited?"

"Not anymore. They're working it out, Cami says. She's cautiously optimistic."

For a moment, the ache inside him eased a little, to learn that Cami hadn't lost her father, after all.

Nell said way too damn smugly, "You know one way or another, Ma is going find a way to get a little quality time with you."

"Yeah, well. She'll have to catch me first."

Garrett managed to avoid his mother for four full days. But then on Wednesday, exactly one week after Cami moved out, he made the mistake of going home before midnight. He'd stopped for takeout at Romano's and got home at a little after eight—and he was sitting at the kitchen island shoveling in spaghetti carbonara when the doorbell rang.

The funny thing was, he knew it was Willow. He could have just refused to answer the door.

But getting home earlier hadn't really been a mistake. He'd survived a whole week without Cami.

It was a week too long.

He had to do something, find a way to say the things he'd sworn he would never say to any woman ever again. Maybe Ma could help him with that.

But even if she couldn't, he was ready to listen to her tell him what a damn fool he'd been.

He went to the door and let her in. "Want some spaghetti?"

"I ate with Griff."

She said she'd take coffee, so he made them each a cup. It was a nice night. He led her out to the table on the lower deck. Munch sniffed the bushes for a while, then came and stretched out beside Willow's chair.

She stuck her hand down and scratched his head—and then got right to business. "You sent that sweet girl away?"

Coffee sloshed as he set his cup down too forcefully. "No. I never wanted her to go. I just want her with me. Like, permanently."

"You're making no sense, Garrett. That girl's in love with you. She wouldn't leave you unless you did something to make her go."

He moved his mug to the left and then slid it to the right again. "When things went south with Miranda, I kind of gave up on love." His mother laughed. Sometimes she was the most insensitive person on the planet. "It's not funny, Ma."

"Wait till you're my age. You'll get the humor."

"The thing is, Cami said she loved me. I told her I wasn't going there, so she moved out. She says she can't be my friend, not for a while, not till she gets over me, or whatever."

"Is that really what you want from her, for her to get over you so that she can be your *friend*?"

"I just want her, okay? I just…want to be with her, take care of her, eat lunch with her, hear about her damn day."

Ma rested her forearm on the table. That gigantic diamond Griffin had given her glittered in the fading light. "Garrett, you're in love with her."

He drank some coffee and set the cup down with a little more care that time. "Yeah. I am. I really am."

When the doorbell rang at a quarter after nine that night, Cami was alone in the loft. She assumed the unexpected guest was some friend of Nell's, but she checked the peephole just to be safe.

Her heart leaped into her throat and got stuck there when she saw it was Garrett. Hope bloomed.

And then died an ugly death.

No way could she let herself get her hopes up just to get them crushed to dust all over again.

Garrett tapped on the other side of the door. "Cami." His voice was slightly muffled, but she heard him well enough. "I know you're in there. Let me in."

She pressed her hands to the door, laid her cheek against it and shut her eyes. It almost felt like being close to him again—just to know he was on the other side.

Whatever he'd really come here for.

"What do you want, Garrett? I told you I didn't want to see you for a while."

"Cami. Come on." His voice, so gruff and deep and thrilling, destroyed her. Another shimmer of longing shuddered through her. It hurt so much it almost felt good. "Open the door."

The yearning was too strong. She gave in and pulled back the door. The sight of him broke her poor heart all over again.

She couldn't do this. Whatever he wanted, she couldn't deal with it right now.

He caught the door before she could shut it in his face. "Let me in. Please. I've got stuff to say. Just hear me out." His hair was as thick and unruly as ever. And those melty eyes turned her knees to mush. He looked kind of tired. She supposed that she did, too. Sleeping wasn't that easy without his big arms to hold her.

She stepped back, clearing the way for him, though she knew she shouldn't.

And then he was inside with her, bringing the too-tempting scent of his skin and all that electricity he generated for her, just by being him. Having him right there in front of her was so hard to bear. She retreated another step, and he shut the door.

What was she supposed to say? "You want something to drink or—?"

"Nothing. Just to talk."

"Well, all right." The living area was one big, high-ceilinged space. She led him over to the sofa and chairs near the floor-to-ceiling front windows. "Have a seat." He took one end of the sofa. She backed to a chair and sat down, too. "Now. What?"

His gaze was all over her, making slow passes from her bare feet up her legs to her cutoffs and the plaid shirt she'd tied in a knot at her waist. "You look so beautiful."

Her hand went to her hair. She had no idea why. "You came here to tell me I'm beautiful?"

He didn't answer. He just stared at her in that hungry, sexy way he had that always made her want to rip off her clothes and jump in his lap.

She demanded, "Garrett, what are you *doing*?"

He seemed to shake himself. "Nell said your dad called and he wants to make things right."

"Yeah. He, um, I think he's finally accepted that my life is my own. I'm meeting him and Mom for din-

ner next week and they will be coming to my grand
opening in October."

"That's so great. I'm glad."

They stared at each other. Her heart raced and
her breathing sounded ragged and way too loud. She
clutched the chair cushion to keep from leaping up and
throwing herself at him. "Please. What's this about?"

He didn't answer right away. She was about to ask
the question again when he finally said, "It's been a
week since you left me."

"I know that. I've lived through it, too."

"You were right to leave."

"Seriously, Garrett? You think I needed you to
come here and tell me that?"

"Probably not. But it's been a week of hell. I work
and I work some more and then I fall into bed and I
can't sleep. Munch is really pissed at me."

"Is he okay?"

"He'll live. He just misses you. *I* miss you. It's kill-
ing me. But I... You were right to go because you deserve the truth from me and I wasn't willing to give
you that a week ago. I was holding on to old garbage
and I needed to let all that crap go."

"What garbage?" It came out as a croak.

"The garbage that I wasn't going to go there again,
that I would never try to love someone again, because
I'm so bad at it and I would only mess it up. I didn't
want to mess it up with you, Cami. But somehow, I
went and did it anyway. I messed it up and all for nothing. Because I lost you *and* I love you. And I think I
always will."

She realized she'd stopped breathing. "Excuse me.
What did you just say?"

"I said I love you, Cami. God, you have no idea how much. It feels like I've loved you since the first minute I saw you, standing there in your poufy white dress looking like you'd just gone a few rounds with Muhammad Ali. I saw you and I was finished, done for, just like in all those corny romantic movies. You're the one for me."

"I… You… Garrett, did you hear yourself? You just said you love me."

"Because I do. I love you, Cami. I belong to you. Please come back to me. Please be mine and I'll be yours and we won't let anything ever tear us apart."

That did it.

With a cry of sheer gladness, she leaped from her chair. He got up, too.

"Garrett, you mean it? I can come home?"

"Please, Cami. Please come home." And he held out his arms to her.

It was all the encouragement she needed. She threw herself at him. He caught her in flight. She wrapped her arms and legs around him good and tight and pressed a big smack of a kiss on his scruffy cheek. "That does it. You'll never get rid of me now."

"Excellent." He looked at her with such tenderness, with the same love and longing she felt in her soul. "Because I don't want to live without you. I want you there in our bed when we wake up in the morning. I want to bring home the takeout and share it with you. I want it all with you, Cami. I want a lifetime, you and me."

And then he kissed her.

Oh, the feel of his lips on hers. Nothing could ever

compare to that. She surrendered to that kiss with her whole heart, holding nothing back.

And when he lifted his head, she said, "Forever? You really mean it?"

"I do."

"What about kids? I do want kids someday."

"I never thought I would again. But now, with you…" He gave her that slow smile, the one that set the butterflies loose in her belly. "Yeah. Kids. I want them, too."

"You would? Really?"

"Cami, with you, I want what you said you wanted a week ago—everything." And then he said, "Marry me."

And she said, "Yes."

He demanded, "Right away."

"Absolutely. I want it outdoors, Garrett. I want it easy and casual. With a picnic reception after."

He kissed her again, long and slow and sweet. And then he nuzzled her ear and whispered, "I know just the place."

They were married on Moosejaw Mountain eleven days later, on the second Saturday in September.

The whole Bravo family drove up to the cabin for the ceremony. The Lockwoods came, too. It was a beautiful day, warm for September. The endless Colorado sky was cloudless and a slight breeze stirred the evergreens.

Cami wore a white sundress with a handkerchief hem and white flip-flops on her feet. She had a crown of flowers in her hair and carried a bouquet of black-eyed Susans. Her father walked her down the make-shift aisle between the rows of folding chairs to where Garrett waited for her, so handsome in jeans, a white shirt and a tan vest. Munch, looking dapper in a black satin bow tie, sat proudly at his side.

Garrett held out his hands to her. She took them. Facing each other, hands clasped, they said their vows—to love, to honor and to cherish, for the rest of their lives.

As the minister declared them husband and wife, Cami knew that running away from marriage to the wrong man had been the smartest thing she'd ever done. Now she would never have to run away again. She had found her true home at last in Garrett Bravo's loving arms.

* * * * *

*Nell Bravo is the only single Bravo left
in Justice Creek, Colorado.
But not for long. Declan McGrath is determined
to claim her, even if he has to break a few rules
to make her his.*

*Don't miss the final installment of
THE BRAVOS OF JUSTICE CREEK,
MARRIED TILL CHRISTMAS,
coming in December 2017
wherever Harlequin Special Edition books
and ebooks are sold.*

*And catch up with the rest of the Bravo family:
THE LAWMAN'S CONVENIENT BRIDE
A BRAVO FOR CHRISTMAS
MS. BRAVO AND THE BOSS
available now from Harlequin Special Edition!*

*Julia Winston is looking to conquer life,
not become heartbreaker Jamie Caine's
latest conquest. But when two young brothers
wind up in Julia's care for the holidays,
she'll take any help she can get—even Jamie's.*

Read on for a preview of
New York Times *bestselling author
RaeAnne Thayne's* SUGAR PINE TRAIL,
the latest installment in her beloved
HAVEN POINT *series..*

CHAPTER ONE

THIS WAS GOING to be a disaster.

Julia Winston stood in her front room looking out the lace curtains framing her bay window at the gleaming black SUV parked in her driveway like a sleek, predatory beast.

Her stomach jumped with nerves, and she rubbed suddenly clammy hands down her skirt. Under what crazy moon had she ever thought this might be a good idea? She must have been temporarily out of her head.

Those nerves jumped into overtime when a man stepped out of the vehicle and stood for a moment, looking up at her house.

Jamie Caine.

Tall, lean, hungry.

Gorgeous.

Now the nerves felt more like nausea. What had

she done? The moment Eliza Caine called and asked her if her brother-in-law could rent the upstairs apartment of Winston House, she should have told her friend in no uncertain terms that the idea was preposterous. Utterly impossible.

As usual, Julia had been weak and indecisive, and when Eliza told her it was only for six weeks—until January, when the condominium Jamie Caine was buying in a new development along the lake would be finished—she had wavered.

He needed a place to live, and she *did* need the money. Anyway, it was only for six weeks. Surely she could tolerate having the man living upstairs in her apartment for six weeks—especially since he would be out of town for much of those six weeks as part of his duties as lead pilot for the Caine Tech company jet fleet.

The reality of it all was just beginning to sink in, though. Jamie Caine, upstairs from her, in all his sexy, masculine glory.

She fanned herself with her hand, wondering if she was having a premature-onset hot flash or if her new furnace could be on the fritz. The temperature in here seemed suddenly off the charts.

How would she tolerate having him here, spending her evenings knowing he was only a few steps away and that she would have to do her best to hide the absolutely ridiculous, truly humiliating crush she had on the man?

This was such a mistake.

Heart pounding, she watched through the frothy curtains as he pulled a long black duffel bag from the back of his SUV and slung it over his shoulder, lifted a laptop case over the other shoulder, then closed the cargo door and headed for the front steps.

A moment later, her old-fashioned musical doorbell echoed through the house. If she hadn't been so nervous, she might have laughed at the instant reaction of the three cats, previously lounging in various states of boredom around the room. The moment the doorbell rang, Empress and Tabitha both jumped off the sofa as if an electric current had just zipped through it, while Audrey Hepburn arched her back and bushed out her tail.

"That's right, girls. We've got company. It's a man, believe it or not, and he's moving in upstairs. Get ready."

The cats sniffed at her with their usual disdainful look. Empress ran in front of her, almost tripping her on the way to answer the door—on purpose, she was quite sure.

With her mother's cats darting out ahead of her, Julia walked out into what used to be the foyer of the house before she had created the upstairs apartment and now served as an entryway to both residences. She opened the front door, doing her best to ignore the rapid tripping of her heartbeat.

"Hi. You're Julia, right?"

As his sister-in-law was one of her dearest friends, she and Jamie had met numerous times at various events at Snow Angel Cove and elsewhere, but she didn't bother reminding him of that. Julia knew she was eminently forgettable. Most of the time, that was just the way she liked it.

"Yes. Hello, Mr. Caine."

He aimed his high-wattage killer smile at her. "Please. Jamie. Nobody calls me Mr. Caine."

Julia was grimly aware of her pulse pounding in her ears and a strange hitch in her lungs. Up close, Jamie Caine was, in a word, breathtaking. He was Mr. Darcy, Atticus Finch, Rhett Butler and Tom Cruise in *Top Gun* all rolled into one glorious package.

Dark hair, blue eyes and that utterly charming Caine smile he shared with Aidan, Eliza's husband, and the other Caine brothers she had met at various events.

"You were expecting me, right?" he said after an awkward pause. She jolted, suddenly aware she was staring and had left him standing entirely too long on her front step. She was an idiot. "Yes. Of course. Come in. I'm sorry."

Pull yourself together. He's just a guy who happens to be gorgeous.

So far she was seriously failing at Landlady 101. She sucked in a breath and summoned her most brisk keep-your-voice-down-please librarian persona.

"As you can see, we will share the entry. Because the home is on the registry of historical buildings, I couldn't put in an outside entrance to your apartment, as I might have preferred. The house was built in 1880, one of the earliest brick homes on Lake Haven. It was constructed by an ancestor of mine, Sir Robert Winston, who came from a wealthy British family and made his own fortune supplying timber to the railroads. He also invested in one of the first hot-springs resorts in the area. The home is Victorian, specifically in the spindled Queen Anne style. It consists of seven bedrooms and four bathrooms. When those bathrooms were added in the 1920s, they provided some of the first indoor plumbing in the region."

"Interesting," he said, though his expression indicated he found it anything but.

She was rambling, she realized, as she tended to do when she was nervous.

She cleared her throat and pointed to the doorway, where the three cats were lined up like sentinels, watching him with unblinking stares. "Anyway, through those doors is my apartment and yours is upstairs. I have keys to both doors for you along with a packet of information here."

She glanced toward the ornate marble-top table in the entryway—that her mother claimed once graced the mansion of Leland Stanford on Nob Hill in San Francisco—where she thought she had left the information. Unfortunately, it was bare. "Oh. Where did I put that? I must have left it inside in my living room. Just a moment."

The cats weren't inclined to get out of her way, so she stepped over them, wondering if she came across as eccentric to him as she felt, a spinster librarian living with cats in a crumbling house crammed with antiques, a space much too big for one person.

After a mad scan of the room, she finally found the two keys along with the carefully prepared file folder of instructions atop the mantel, nestled amid her collection of porcelain angels. She had no recollection of moving them there, probably due to her own nervousness at having Jamie Caine moving upstairs.

She swooped them up and hurried back to the entry, where she found two of the cats curled around his leg, while Audrey was in his arms, currently being petted by his long, square-tipped fingers.

She stared. The cats had no time or interest in her.

She only kept them around because her mother had adored them, and Julia couldn't bring herself to give away Mariah's adored pets. Apparently no female—human or feline—was immune to Jamie Caine. She should have expected it.

"Nice cats."

Julia frowned. "Not usually. They're standoffish and bad tempered to most people."

"I guess I must have the magic touch."

So the Haven Point rumor mill said about him, anyway. "I guess you do," she said. "I found your keys and information about the apartment. If you would like, I can show you around upstairs."

"Lead on."

He offered a friendly smile, and she told herself that shiver rippling down her spine was only because the entryway was cooler than her rooms.

"This is a lovely house," he said as he followed her up the staircase. "Have you lived here long?"

"Thirty-two years in February. All my life, in other words."

Except the first few days, anyway, when she had still been in the Oregon hospital where her parents adopted her, and the three years she had spent at Boise State.

"It's always been in my family," she continued. "My father was born here and his father before him."

She was a Winston only by adoption but claimed her parents' family trees as her own and respected and admired their ancestors and the elegant home they had built here.

At the second-floor landing, she unlocked the apartment that had been hers until she moved down to take care of her mother after Mariah's first stroke, two years ago. A few years after taking the job at the Haven Point library, she had redecorated the upstairs floor of the house. It had been her way of carving out her own space.

Yes, she had been an adult living with her parents. Even as she might have longed for some degree of independence, she couldn't justify moving out when her mother had so desperately needed her help with Julia's ailing father.

Anyway, she had always figured it wasn't the same as most young adults who lived in their parents' apartments. She'd had an entire self-contained floor to herself. If she wished, she could shop on her own, cook on her own, entertain her friends, all without bothering her parents.

Really, it had been the best of all situations—close enough to help, yet removed enough to live her own life. Then her father died and her mother became frail herself, and Julia had felt obligated to move downstairs to be closer, in case her mother needed her.

Now, as she looked at her once-cherished apartment, she tried to imagine how Jamie Caine would see these rooms, with the graceful reproduction furniture and the pastel wall colors and the soft carpet and curtains.

Oddly, the feminine decorations only served to emphasize how very *male* Jamie Caine was, in contrast.

She did her best to ignore that unwanted observation.

"This is basically the same floor plan as my rooms below, with three bedrooms, as well as the living room and kitchen," she explained. "You've got an en suite bathroom off the largest bedroom and another one for the other two bedrooms."

"Wow. That's a lot of room for one guy."

"It's a big house," she said with a shrug. She had even more room downstairs, factoring in the extra bedroom in one addition and the large south-facing sunroom.

Winston House was entirely too rambling for one single woman and three bad-tempered cats. It had been too big for an older couple and their adopted daughter. It had been too large when it was just her and her mother, after her father died.

The place had basically echoed with emptiness for the better part of a year after her mother's deteriorating condition had necessitated her move to the nursing home in Shelter Springs. Her mother had hoped to return to the house she had loved, but that never happened, and Mariah Winston died four months ago.

Julia missed her every single day.

"Do you think it will work for you?" she asked.

"It's more than I need, but should be fine. Eliza told you this is only temporary, right?"

Julia nodded. She was counting on it. Then she could find a nice, quiet, older lady to rent who wouldn't leave her so nervous.

"She said your apartment lease ran out before your new condo was finished."

"Yes. The development was supposed to be done two months ago, but the builder has suffered delay after delay. I've already extended my lease twice. I didn't want to push my luck with my previous landlady by asking for a third extension."

All Jamie had to do was smile at the woman and she likely would have extended his lease again without quibbling. And probably would have given him anything else he wanted, too.

Julia didn't ask why he chose not to move into

Snow Angel Cove with his brother Aidan and Aidan's wife, Eliza, and their children. It was none of her business, anyway. The only thing she cared about was the healthy amount he was paying her in rent, which would just about cover the new furnace she had installed a month earlier.

"It was a lucky break for me when Eliza told me you were considering taking on a renter for your upstairs space."

He aimed that killer smile at her again, and her core muscles trembled from more than just her workout that morning.

If she wasn't very, very careful, she would end up making a fool of herself over the man.

It took effort, but she fought the urge to return his smile. This was business, she told herself. That was all. She had something he needed, a place to stay, and he was willing to pay for it. She, in turn, needed funds if she wanted to maintain this house that had been in her family for generations.

"It works out for both of us. You've already signed the rental agreement outlining the terms of your tenancy and the rules."

She held out the information packet. "Here you'll find all the information you might need, information like internet access, how to work the electronics and the satellite television channels, garbage pickup day and mail delivery. Do you have any other questions?"

Business, she reminded herself, making her voice as no-nonsense and brisk as possible.

"I can't think of any now, but I'm sure something will come up."

He smiled again, but she thought perhaps this time

his expression was a little more reserved. Maybe he could sense she was un-charmable.

Or so she wanted to tell herself, anyway.

"I would ask that you please wipe your feet when you carry your things in and out, given the snow out there. The stairs are original wood, more than a hundred years old."

Cripes. She sounded like a prissy spinster librarian.

"I will do that, but I don't have much to carry in. Since El told me the place is furnished, I put almost everything in storage." He gestured to the duffel and laptop bag, which he had set inside the doorway. "Besides this, I've only got a few more boxes in the car."

"In that case, here are your keys. The large one goes to the outside door. The smaller one is for your apartment. I keep the outside door locked at all times. You can't be too careful."

"True enough."

She glanced at her watch. "I'm afraid I've already gone twenty minutes past my lunch hour and must return to the library. My cell number is written on the front of the packet, in case of emergency."

"Looks like you've covered everything."

"I think so." Yes, she was a bit obsessively organized, and she didn't like surprises. Was anything wrong with that?

"I hope you will be comfortable here," she said, then tried to soften her stiff tone with a smile that felt every bit as awkward. "Good afternoon."

"Uh, same to you."

Her heart was still pounding as she nodded to him and hurried for the stairs, desperate for escape from all that...masculinity.

She rushed back downstairs and into her apartment for her purse, wishing she had time to splash cold water on her face.

However would she get through the next six weeks with him in her house?

HE WAS *NOT* looking forward to the next six weeks.

Jamie stood in the corner of the main living space to the apartment he had agreed to rent, sight unseen.

Big mistake.

It was roomy and filled with light, that much was true. But the decor was too…fussy…for a man like him, all carved wood and tufted upholstery and pastel wall colorings.

It wasn't exactly his scene, more like the kind of place a repressed, uppity librarian might live.

As soon as he thought the words, Jamie frowned at himself. That wasn't fair. She might not have been overflowing with warmth and welcome, but Julia Winston had been very polite to him—especially since he knew she hadn't necessarily wanted to rent to him.

This was what happened when he gave his sister-in-law free rein to find him an apartment in the tight local rental market. She had been helping him out, since he had been crazy busy the last few weeks flying Caine Tech execs from coast to coast—and all places in between—as they worked on a couple of big mergers.

Eliza had wanted him to stay at her and Aidan's rambling house by the lake. The place was huge, and they had plenty of room, but while he loved his older brother Aidan and his wife and kids, Jamie preferred his own space. He didn't much care what that space looked like, especially when it was temporary.

With time running out on his lease extension, he had been relieved when Eliza called him via Skype the week before to tell him she had found him something more than suitable, for a decent rent.

"You'll love it!" Eliza had beamed. "It's the entire second floor of a gorgeous old Victorian in that great neighborhood on Snow Blossom Lane, with a simply stunning view of the lake."

"Sounds good," he had answered.

"You'll be upstairs from my friend Julia Winston, and, believe me, you couldn't ask for a better landlady. She's sweet and kind and perfectly wonderful. You know Julia, right?"

When he had looked blankly at her and didn't immediately respond, his niece Maddie had popped her face into the screen from where she had been apparently listening in off camera. "You know! She's the library lady. She tells all the stories!"

"Ah. *That* Julia," he'd said, not bothering to mention to his seven-year-old niece that in more than a year of living in town, he had somehow missed out on story time at the Haven Point library.

He also didn't mention to Maddie's mother that he only vaguely remembered Julia Winston. Now that he had seen her again, he understood why. She was the kind of woman who tended to slip into the background—and he had the odd impression that wasn't accidental.

She wore her brown hair past her shoulders, without much curl or style to it and held back with a simple black band, and she appeared to use little makeup to play up her rather average features.

She did have lovely eyes, he had to admit. Extraordinary, even. They were a stunning blue, almost violet, fringed by naturally long eyelashes.

Her looks didn't matter, nor did the decor of her house. He would only be here a few weeks, then he would be moving into his new condo.

She clearly didn't like him. He frowned, wondering how he might have offended Julia Winston. He barely remembered even meeting the woman, but he must have done something for her to be so cool to him.

A few times during that odd interaction, she had alternated between seeming nervous to be in the same room with him to looking at him with her mouth pursed tightly, as if she had just caught him spreading peanut butter across the pages of *War and Peace*.

She was entitled to her opinion. Contrary to popular belief, he didn't need everyone to like him.

His brothers would probably say it was good for him to live upstairs from a woman so clearly immune to his charm.

One thing was clear: he now had one more reason to be eager for his condo to be finished.

SUGAR PINE TRAIL
by RaeAnne Thayne
Available October 2017 from HQN Books!

#2581 THE RANCHER'S CHRISTMAS SONG

The Cowboys of Cold Creek • by RaeAnne Thayne

Music teacher Ella Baker doesn't have time to corral rancher Beckett McKinley's two wild boys. But when they ask her to teach them a song for their father, she manages to wrangle some riding lessons out of the deal. Still, Ella and Beckett come from two different worlds, and it might take a Christmas miracle to finally bring them together.

#2582 THE MAVERICK'S SNOWBOUND CHRISTMAS

Montana Mavericks: The Great Family Roundup
by Karen Rose Smith

Rancher Eli Dalton believes that visiting vet Hadley Strickland is just the bride he's been searching for! But can he heal her broken heart in time for the perfect holiday proposal?

#2583 A COWBOY FAMILY CHRISTMAS

Rocking Chair Rodeo • by Judy Duarte

When Drew Madison, a handsome rodeo promoter, meets the temporary cook at the Rocking Chair Ranch, the avowed bachelor falls for the lovely Lainie Montoya. But things get complicated when he learns she's the mystery woman who broke up his sister's marriage!

#2584 SANTA'S SEVEN-DAY BABY TUTORIAL

Hurley's Homestyle Kitchen • by Meg Maxwell

When FBI agent Colt Asher, who's been left with his baby nephews for ten days before Christmas, needs a nanny, he hires Anna Miller, a young Amish woman on *rumspringa* trying to decide if she wants to remain in the outside world or return to her Amish community.

#2585 HIS BY CHRISTMAS

The Bachelors of Blackwater Lake • by Teresa Southwick

Calhoun Hart was planning on filling his forced vacation with adventure and extreme sports until he broke his leg. Now he's stuck on a beautiful tropical island working with Justine Walker to get some business done on the sly— and is suddenly falling for the calm, collected woman with dreams of her own.

#2586 THEIR CHRISTMAS ANGEL

The Colorado Fosters • by Tracy Madison

When widowed single father Parker Lennox falls for his daughters' music teacher, he quickly discovers there's also a baby in the mix—and it isn't his! To complicate matters further, Nicole survived the same cancer that took his wife. Can Santa deliver Parker and Nicole the family they both want for Christmas this year?

YOU CAN FIND MORE INFORMATION ON UPCOMING HARLEQUIN® TITLES, FREE EXCERPTS AND MORE AT WWW.HARLEQUIN.COM.

HSECNM1017

Get 2 Free Books,

HARLEQUIN®

SPECIAL EDITION

Plus 2 Free Gifts—

just for trying the **Reader Service!**

SPECIAL EXCERPT FROM

HARLEQUIN

SPECIAL EDITION

*Ella Baker is trading music lessons for riding
lessons from the wild twin McKinley boys—but it's
their father who would need a Christmas miracle to
let Ella into his heart.*

*Read on for a sneak preview of
the RANCHER'S CHRISTMAS SONG,
the next book in* New York Times *bestselling author*
RaeAnne Thayne*'s beloved miniseries*
THE COWBOYS OF COLD CREEK*.*

Beckett finally spoke. "Uh, what seems to be the trouble?"

His voice had an odd, strangled note to it. Was he
laughing at her? When she couldn't see him, Ella couldn't
be quite sure. "It's stuck in my hair comb. I don't want
to rip the sweater—or yank out my hair, for that matter."

He paused again, then she felt the air stir as he moved
closer. The scent of him was stronger now, masculine and
outdoorsy, and everything inside her sighed a welcome.

He stood close enough that she could feel the heat
radiating from him. She caught her breath, torn between
a completely prurient desire for the moment to last at
least a little longer and a wild hope that the humiliation
of being caught in this position would be over quickly.

"Hold still," he said. Was his voice deeper than usual?
She couldn't quite tell. She did know it sent tiny delicious
shivers down her spine.

"You've really done a job here," he said after a
moment.

"I know. I'm not quite sure how it tangled so badly."

She would have to breathe soon or she was likely to pass out. She forced herself to inhale one breath and then another until she felt a little less light-headed.

"Almost there," he said, his big hands in her hair, then a moment later she felt a tug and the sweater slipped all the way over her head.

"There you go."

"Thank you." She wanted to disappear, to dive under that great big log bed and hide away. Instead, she forced her mouth into a casual smile. "These Christmas sweaters can be dangerous. Who knew?"

She was blushing. She could feel her face heat and wondered if he noticed. This certainly counted among the most embarrassing moments of her life.

"Want to explain again what you're doing in my bedroom, tangled up in your clothes?" he asked.

She frowned at his deliberately risqué interpretation of something that had been innocent. Mostly.

There had been that secret moment when she had closed her eyes and imagined being here with him under that soft quilt, but he had no way of knowing that.

She folded up her sweater, wondering if she would ever be able to look the man in the eye again.

Don't miss
THE RANCHER'S CHRISTMAS SONG
by RaeAnne Thayne,
available November 2017 wherever
Harlequin® Special Edition books and ebooks are sold.

www.Harlequin.com

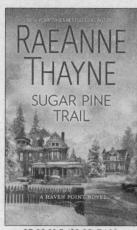

$7.99 U.S./$9.99 CAN.

EXCLUSIVE
Limited Time Offer

$1.⁰⁰ OFF

New York Times Bestselling Author

RaeAnne Thayne

SUGAR PINE TRAIL

An unlikely attraction brings comfort, joy and unforgettable romance this holiday season!

Available September 26, 2017.
Pick up your copy today!

HQN™

$1.⁰⁰ OFF the purchase price of SUGAR PINE TRAIL by RaeAnne Thayne.

Offer valid from September 26, 2017 to October 31, 2017.
Redeemable at participating retail outlets. Not redeemable at Barnes & Noble.
Limit one coupon per purchase. Valid in the U.S.A. and Canada only.

52615030

5 65373 00076 2 (8100)0 12300

THE WORLD IS BETTER WITH

Romance

Harlequin has everything from contemporary, passionate and heartwarming to suspenseful and inspirational stories.

Whatever your mood,
we have a romance just for you!

Connect with us to find your next great read,
special offers and more.

f /HarlequinBooks

🐦 @HarlequinBooks

www.HarlequinBlog.com

www.Harlequin.com/Newsletters

◆ HARLEQUIN®

A *Romance* FOR EVERY MOOD™

www.Harlequin.com